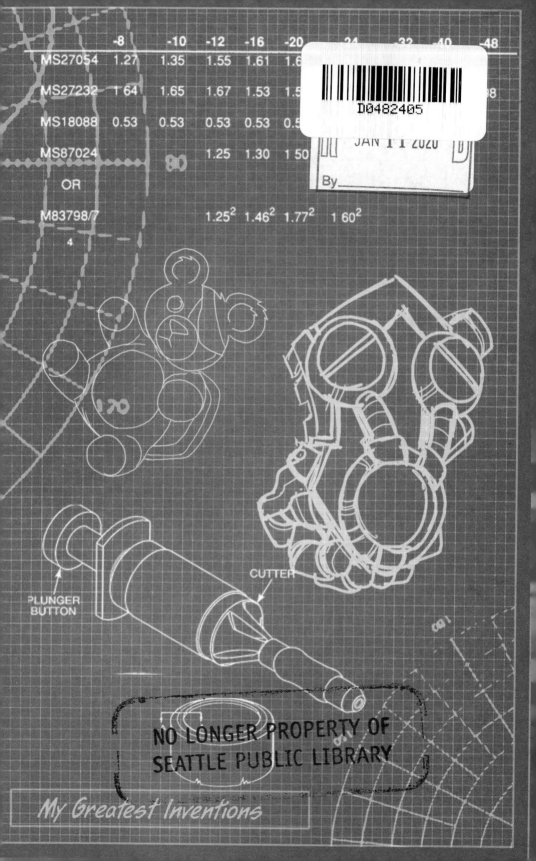

	-8	-10	-12	-16	-20	24	32	40	-48
MS27054	1.27	1.35	1.55	1.61	1.6				
MS27232	1 64	1.65	1.67	1.53	1.5				98
MS18088	0.53	0.53	0.53	0.53	0.5				
MS87024			1.25	1.30	1 50				
OR									
M83798/7			1.25^2	1.46^2	1.77^2	$1 60^2$			
4									

JAN 11 2020

By_____

D0482405

CUTTER

PLUNGER
BUTTON

My Greatest Inventions

THE ONLY LIVING GIRL

THE ISLAND AT THE EDGE OF INFINITY

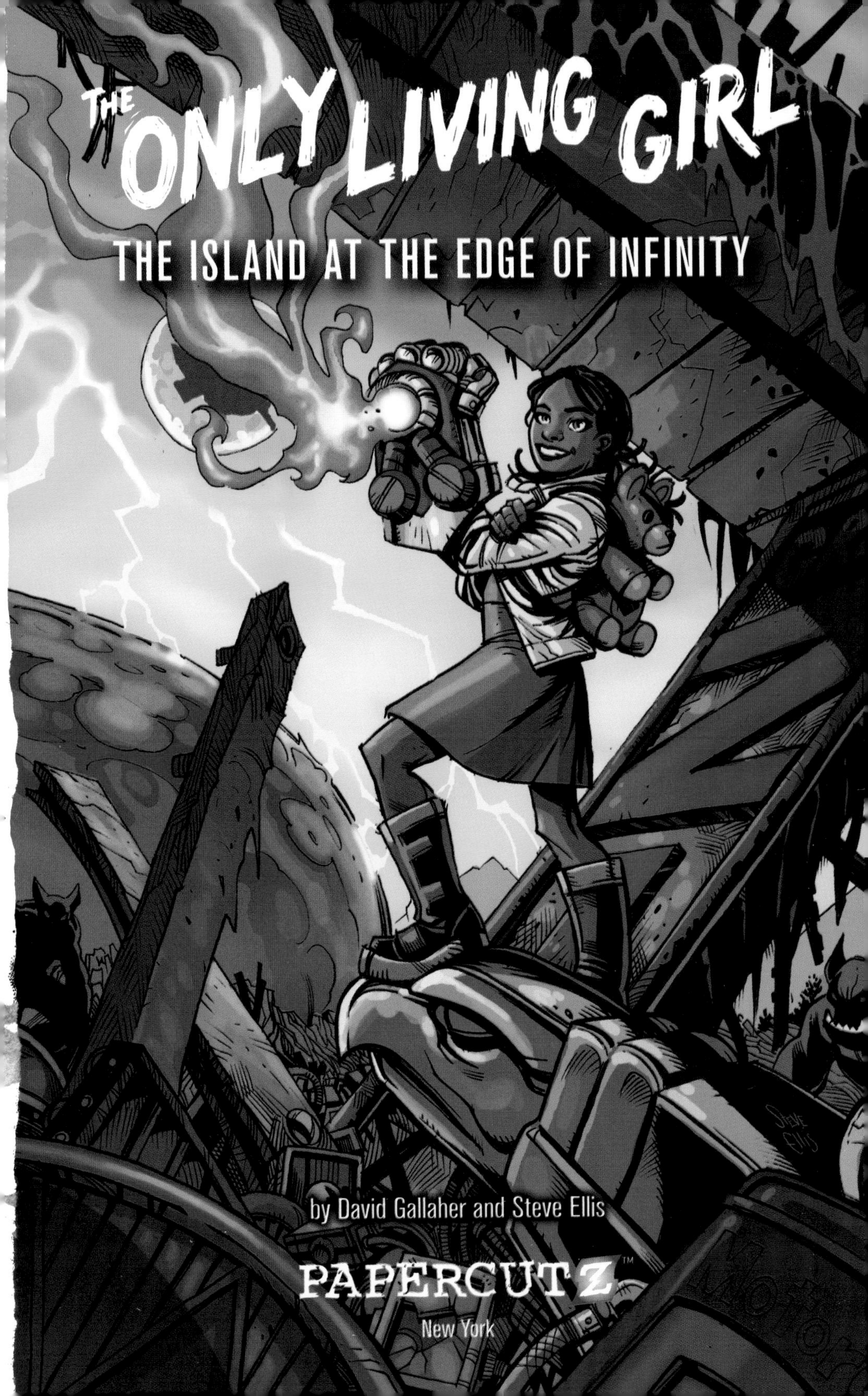
STEVE ELLIS

by David Gallaher and Steve Ellis

PAPERCUTZ™

New York

To my wonderful family, who put up with an artist who is always on crazy deadlines. Thanks for the support, Mila, Jacob and Luna! –Steve

To my family, for their endless support, compassion, and inspiration! –David

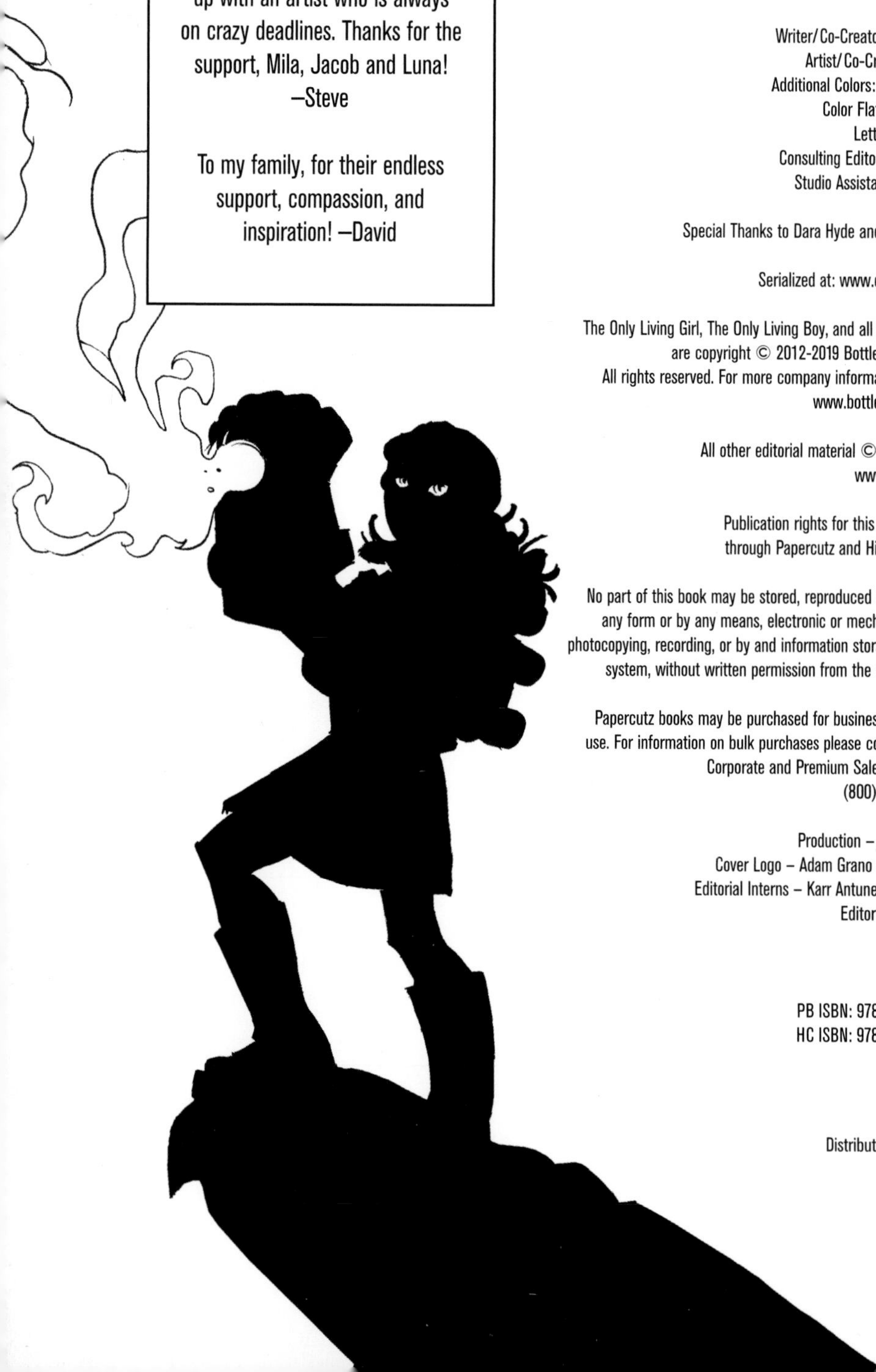

THE ONLY LIVING GIRL #1 "The Island at the Edge of Infinity"

Chapters 1 & 2
Writer/Co-Creator: David Gallaher
Artist/Co-Creator: Steve Ellis
Additional Colors: Chris Sotomayor
Color Flatting: Ryan Leary
Lettering: Nate Pride
Consulting Editor: Janelle Asselin
Studio Assistant: Jen Lightfoot

Special Thanks to Dara Hyde and Vanessa Shealy

Serialized at: www.onlylivinggirl.com

Publication rights for this edition arranged through Papercutz and Hill Nadell Agency.

Production – JayJay Jackson
Cover Logo – Adam Grano and Dawn Guzzo
Editorial Interns – Karr Antunes, Spenser Nellis
Editor – Jeff Whitman
Jim Salicrup
Editor-in-Chief

PB ISBN: 978-1-5458-0202-1
HC ISBN: 978-1-5458-0203-8

Printed in India
April 2019

Distributed by Macmillan
First Printing

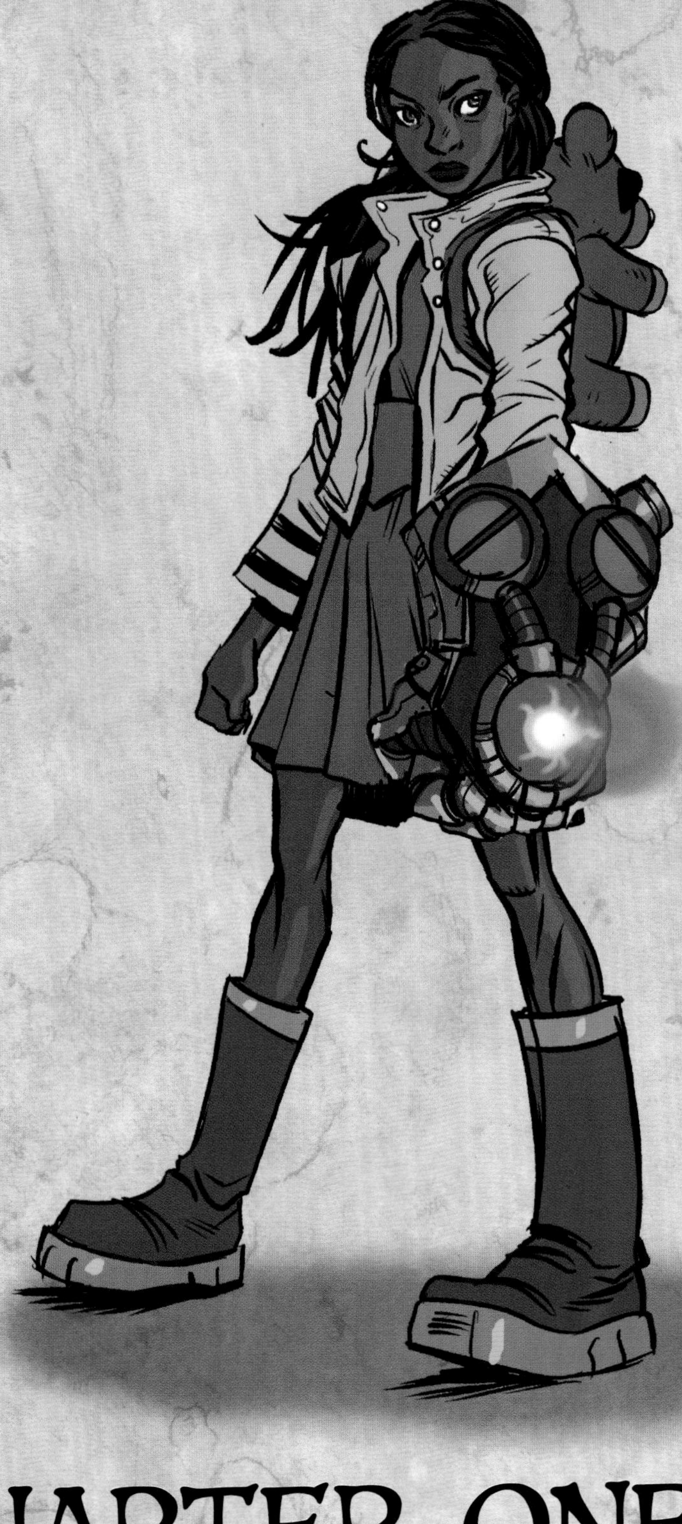

CHAPTER ONE

Previously in...

THE ONLY LIVING BOY

Awake after years of suspended animation, Zandra Parfitt is haunted by memories of her past. Now, as the only living girl left, she must redeem her father's legacy, while trying to survive on a brave new world, where danger and adventure await her.

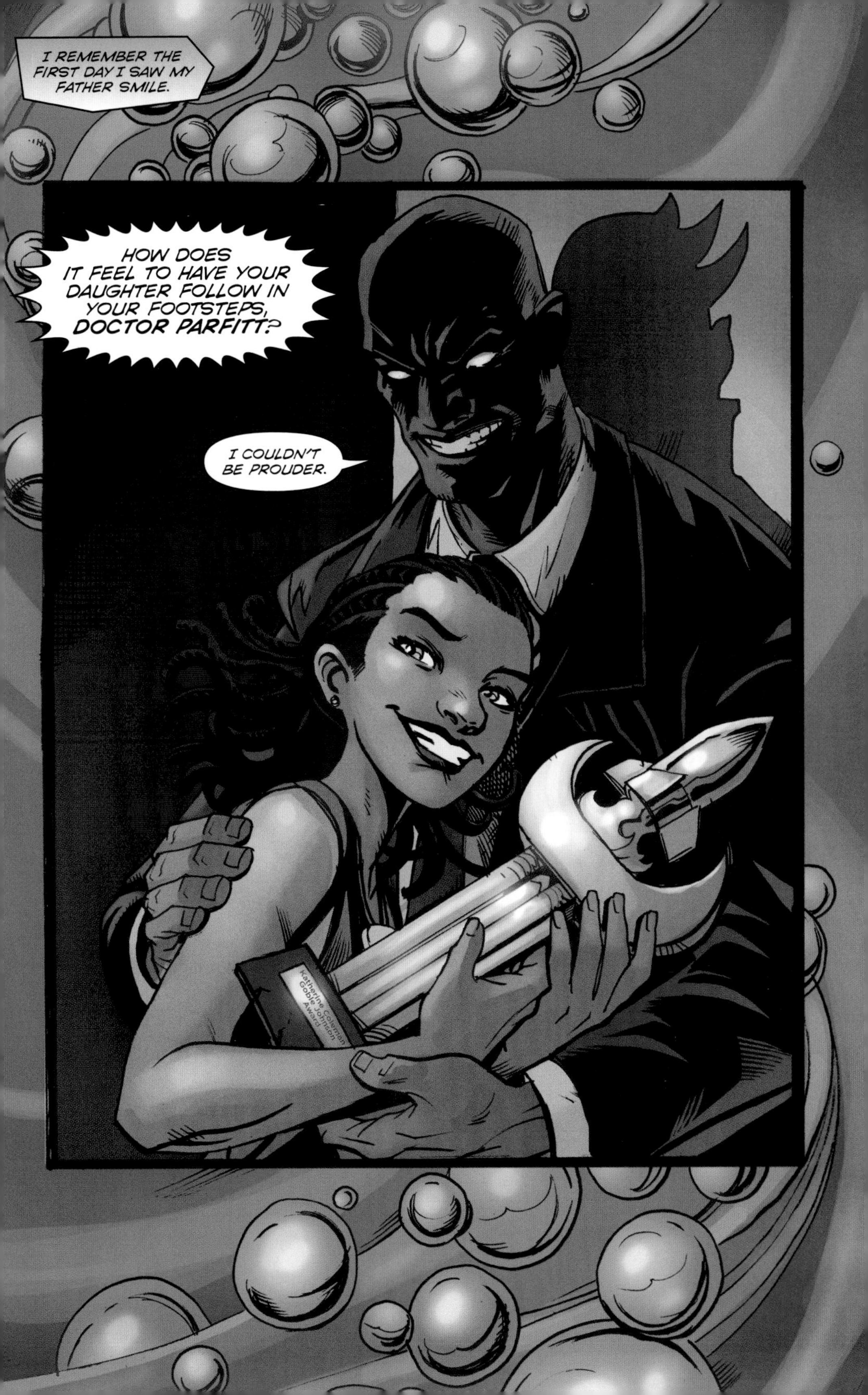
I REMEMBER THE FIRST DAY I SAW MY FATHER SMILE.
HOW DOES IT FEEL TO HAVE YOUR DAUGHTER FOLLOW IN YOUR FOOTSTEPS, DOCTOR PARFITT?
I COULDN'T BE PROUDER.
Katherine Coleman Goble Johnson Award

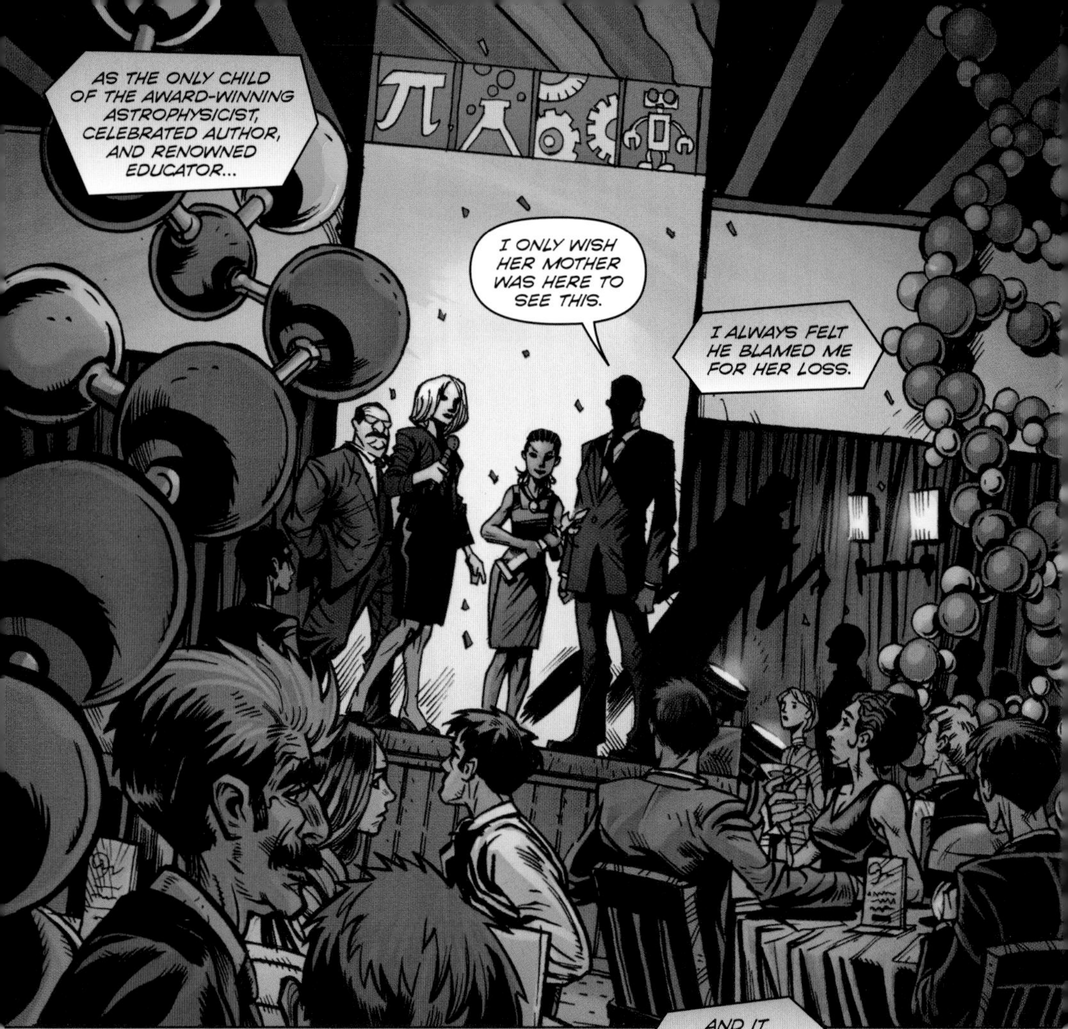
AS THE ONLY CHILD OF THE AWARD-WINNING ASTROPHYSICIST, CELEBRATED AUTHOR, AND RENOWNED EDUCATOR...
I ONLY WISH HER MOTHER WAS HERE TO SEE THIS.
I ALWAYS FELT HE BLAMED ME FOR HER LOSS.

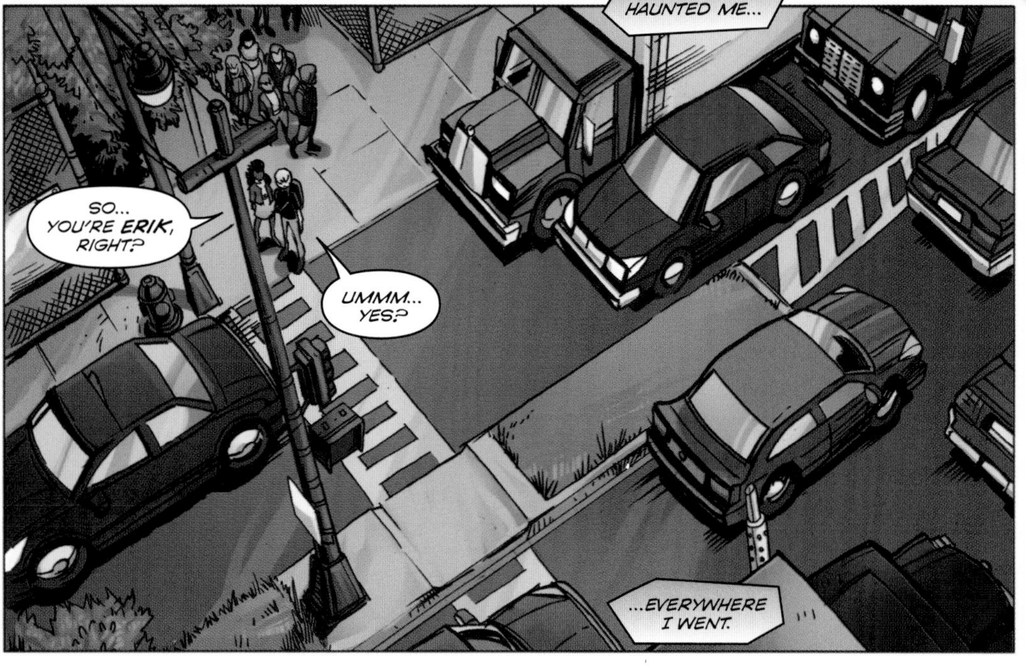
AND IT HAUNTED ME...
SO... YOU'RE ERIK, RIGHT?
UMMM... YES?
...EVERYWHERE I WENT.

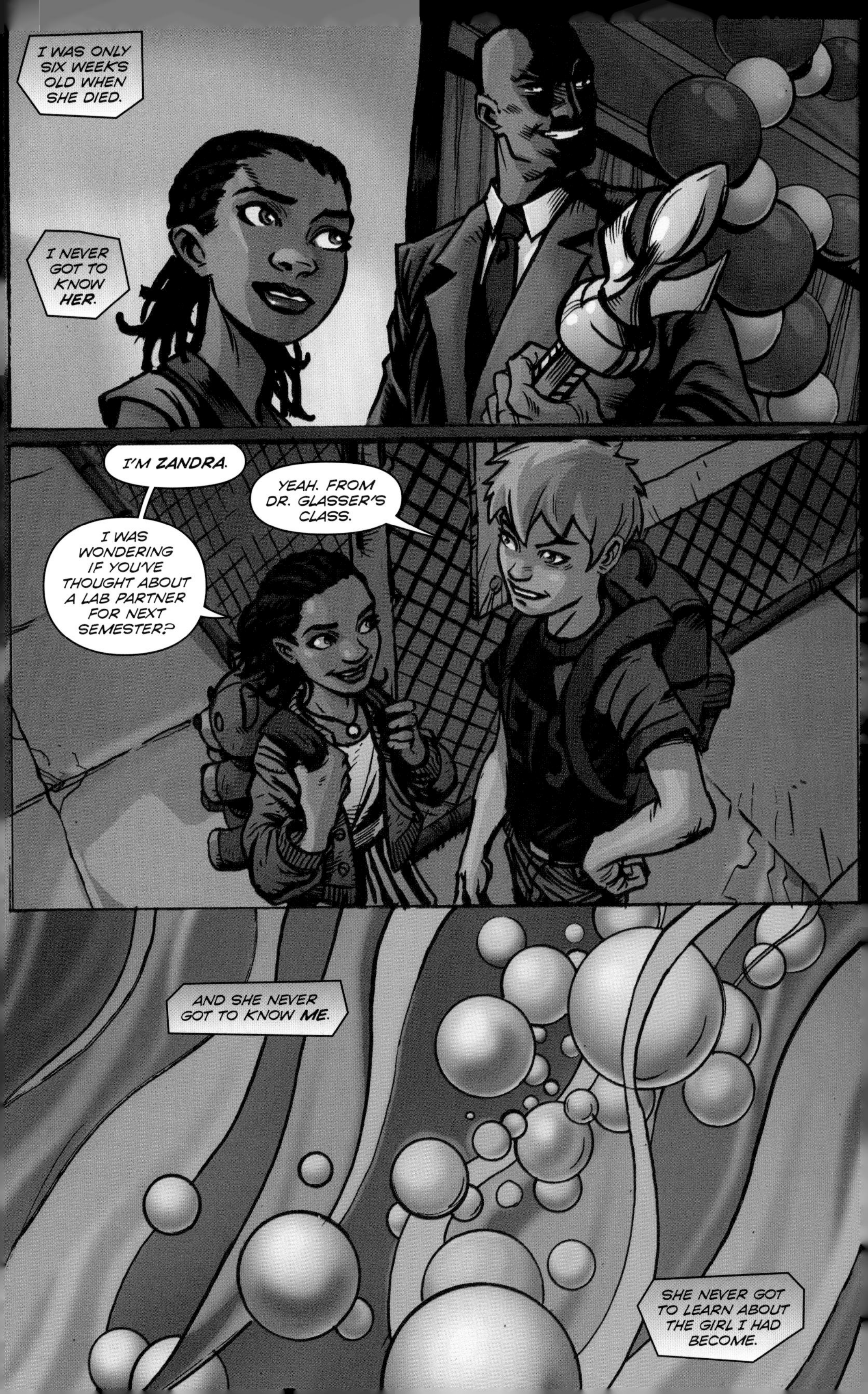
I WAS ONLY SIX WEEKS OLD WHEN SHE DIED.
I NEVER GOT TO KNOW HER.
I'M ZANDRA.
I WAS WONDERING IF YOU'VE THOUGHT ABOUT A LAB PARTNER FOR NEXT SEMESTER?
YEAH. FROM DR. GLASSER'S CLASS.
AND SHE NEVER GOT TO KNOW ME.
SHE NEVER GOT TO LEARN ABOUT THE GIRL I HAD BECOME.

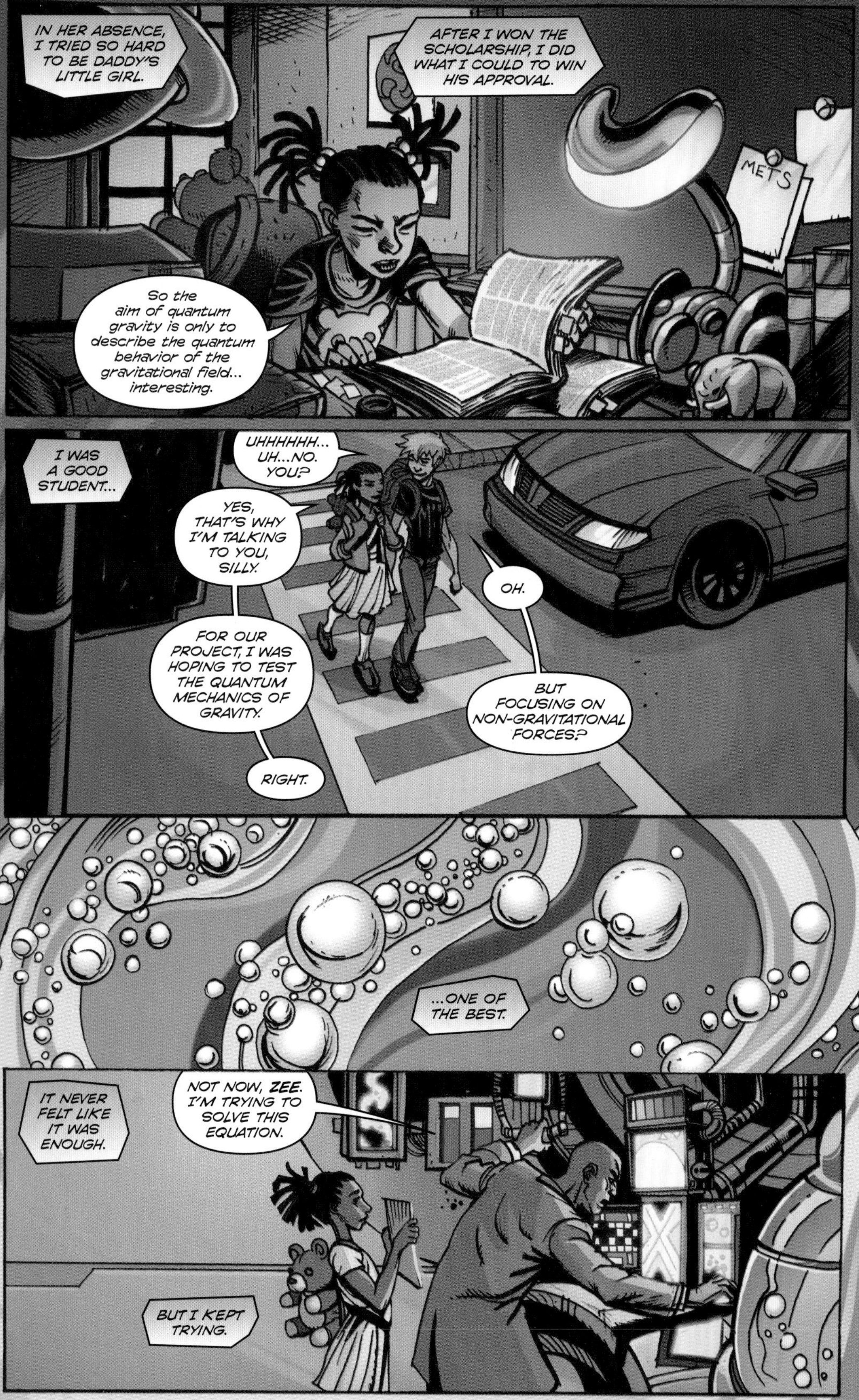
IN HER ABSENCE, I TRIED SO HARD TO BE DADDY'S LITTLE GIRL.
AFTER I WON THE SCHOLARSHIP, I DID WHAT I COULD TO WIN HIS APPROVAL.
METS
So the aim of quantum gravity is only to describe the quantum behavior of the gravitational field... interesting.
I WAS A GOOD STUDENT...
UHHHHHH... UH...NO. YOU?
YES, THAT'S WHY I'M TALKING TO YOU, SILLY.
OH.
FOR OUR PROJECT, I WAS HOPING TO TEST THE QUANTUM MECHANICS OF GRAVITY.
BUT FOCUSING ON NON-GRAVITATIONAL FORCES?
RIGHT.
...ONE OF THE BEST.
IT NEVER FELT LIKE IT WAS ENOUGH.
NOT NOW, ZEE. I'M TRYING TO SOLVE THIS EQUATION.
BUT I KEPT TRYING.

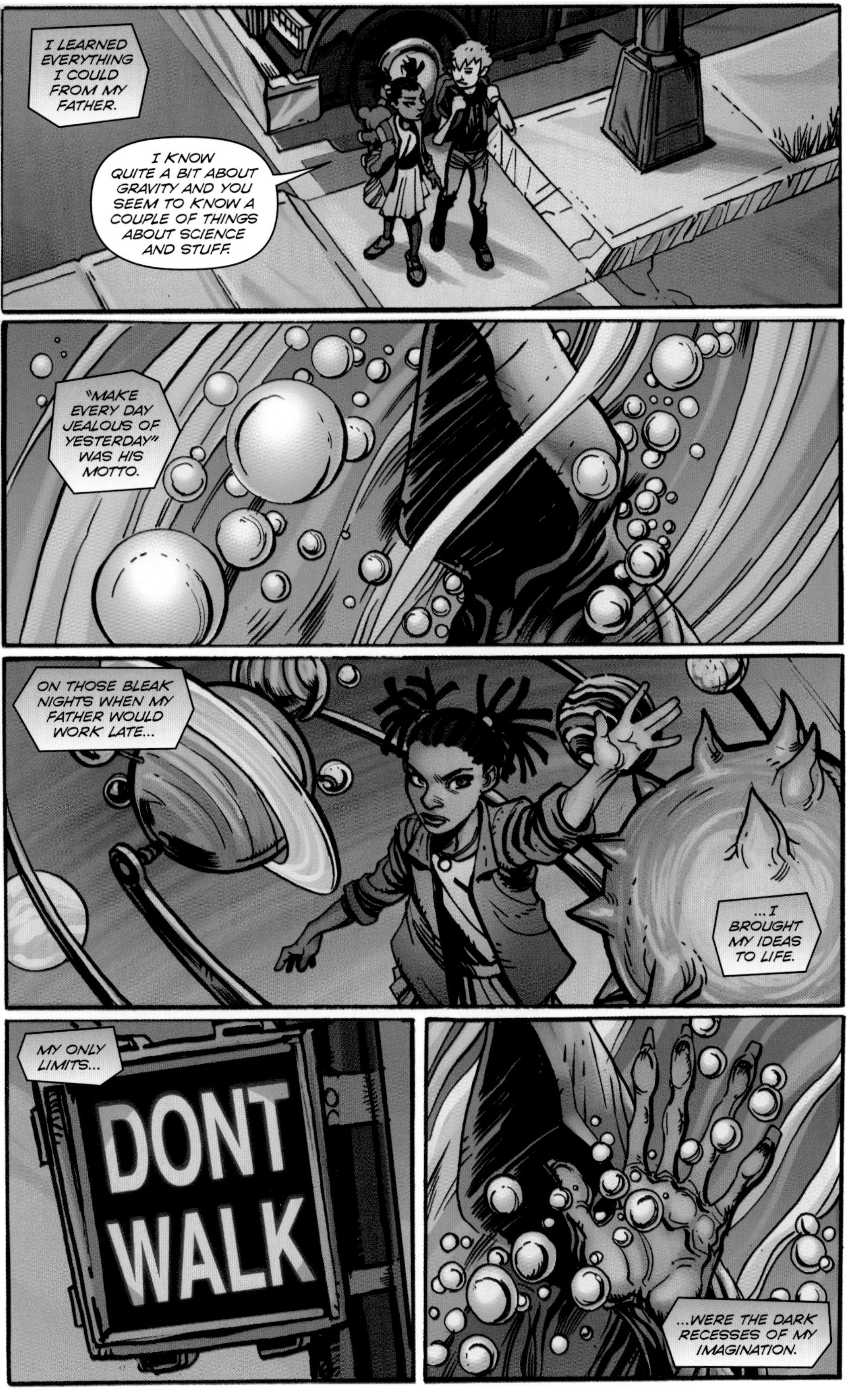
I LEARNED EVERYTHING I COULD FROM MY FATHER.
I KNOW QUITE A BIT ABOUT GRAVITY AND YOU SEEM TO KNOW A COUPLE OF THINGS ABOUT SCIENCE AND STUFF.
"MAKE EVERY DAY JEALOUS OF YESTERDAY" WAS HIS MOTTO.
ON THOSE BLEAK NIGHTS WHEN MY FATHER WOULD WORK LATE...
...I BROUGHT MY IDEAS TO LIFE.
MY ONLY LIMITS...
DONT WALK
...WERE THE DARK RECESSES OF MY IMAGINATION.

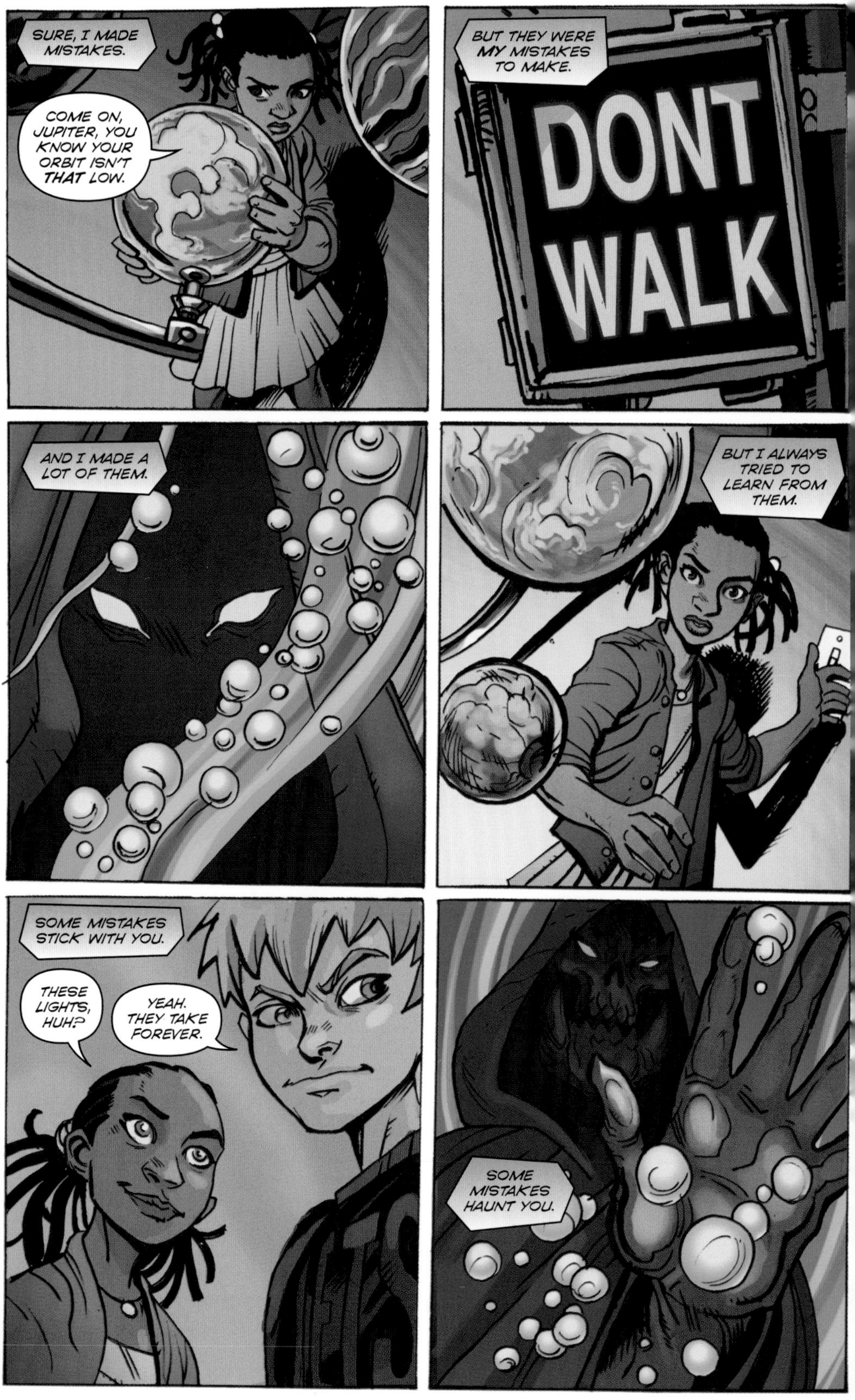
SURE, I MADE MISTAKES.
COME ON, JUPITER, YOU KNOW YOUR ORBIT ISN'T THAT LOW.
BUT THEY WERE MY MISTAKES TO MAKE.
DONT WALK
AND I MADE A LOT OF THEM.
BUT I ALWAYS TRIED TO LEARN FROM THEM.
SOME MISTAKES STICK WITH YOU.
THESE LIGHTS, HUH?
YEAH. THEY TAKE FOREVER.
SOME MISTAKES HAUNT YOU.

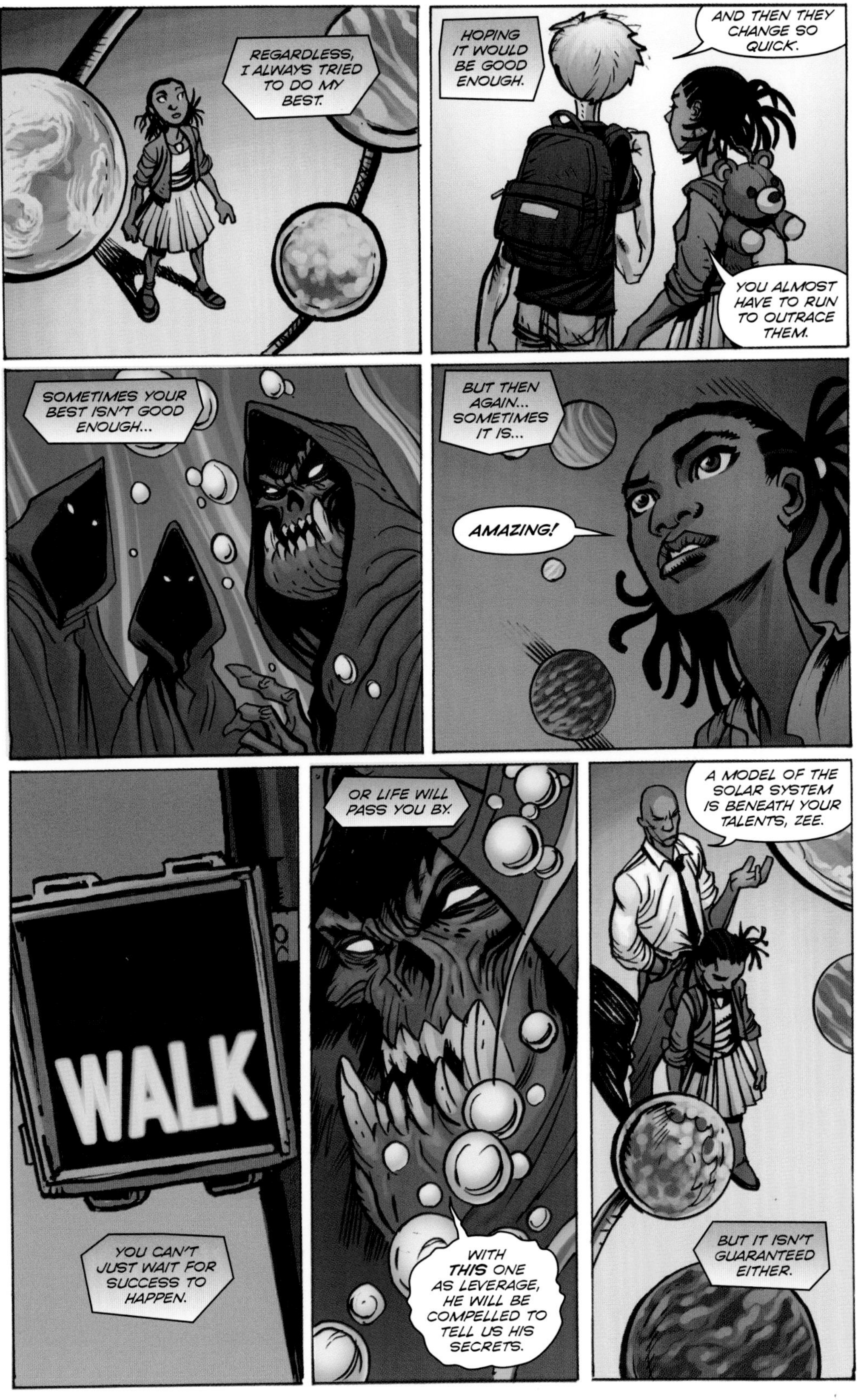
REGARDLESS, I ALWAYS TRIED TO DO MY BEST.
HOPING IT WOULD BE GOOD ENOUGH.
AND THEN THEY CHANGE SO QUICK.
YOU ALMOST HAVE TO RUN TO OUTRACE THEM.
SOMETIMES YOUR BEST ISN'T GOOD ENOUGH...
BUT THEN AGAIN... SOMETIMES IT IS...
AMAZING!
WALK
YOU CAN'T JUST WAIT FOR SUCCESS TO HAPPEN.
OR LIFE WILL PASS YOU BY.
WITH THIS ONE AS LEVERAGE, HE WILL BE COMPELLED TO TELL US HIS SECRETS.
A MODEL OF THE SOLAR SYSTEM IS BENEATH YOUR TALENTS, ZEE.
BUT IT ISN'T GUARANTEED EITHER.

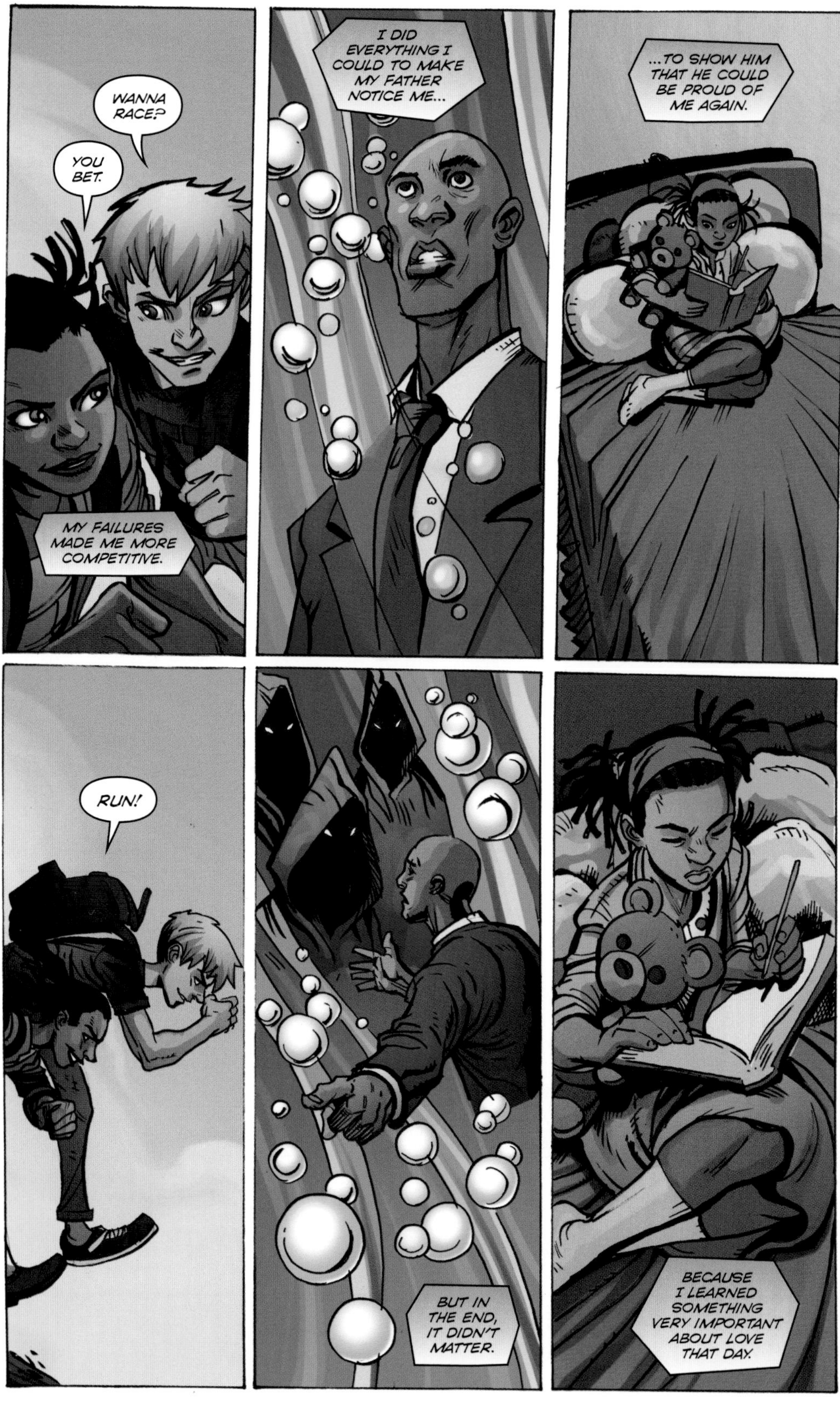
WANNA RACE?
YOU BET.
MY FAILURES MADE ME MORE COMPETITIVE.
I DID EVERYTHING I COULD TO MAKE MY FATHER NOTICE ME...
...TO SHOW HIM THAT HE COULD BE PROUD OF ME AGAIN.
RUN!
BUT IN THE END, IT DIDN'T MATTER.
BECAUSE I LEARNED SOMETHING VERY IMPORTANT ABOUT LOVE THAT DAY.

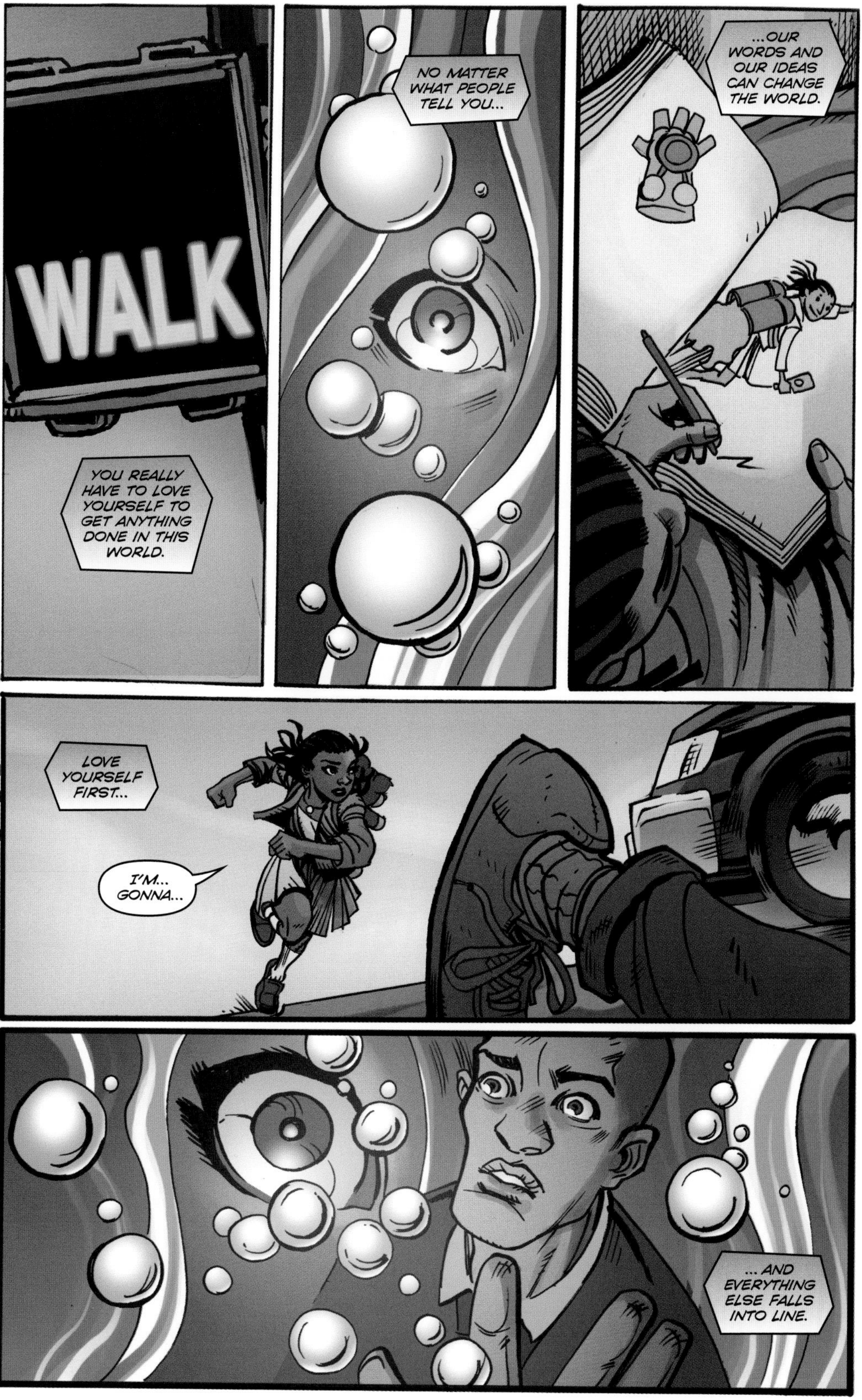
WALK
YOU REALLY HAVE TO LOVE YOURSELF TO GET ANYTHING DONE IN THIS WORLD.
NO MATTER WHAT PEOPLE TELL YOU...
...OUR WORDS AND OUR IDEAS CAN CHANGE THE WORLD.
LOVE YOURSELF FIRST...
I'M... GONNA...
... AND EVERYTHING ELSE FALLS INTO LINE.

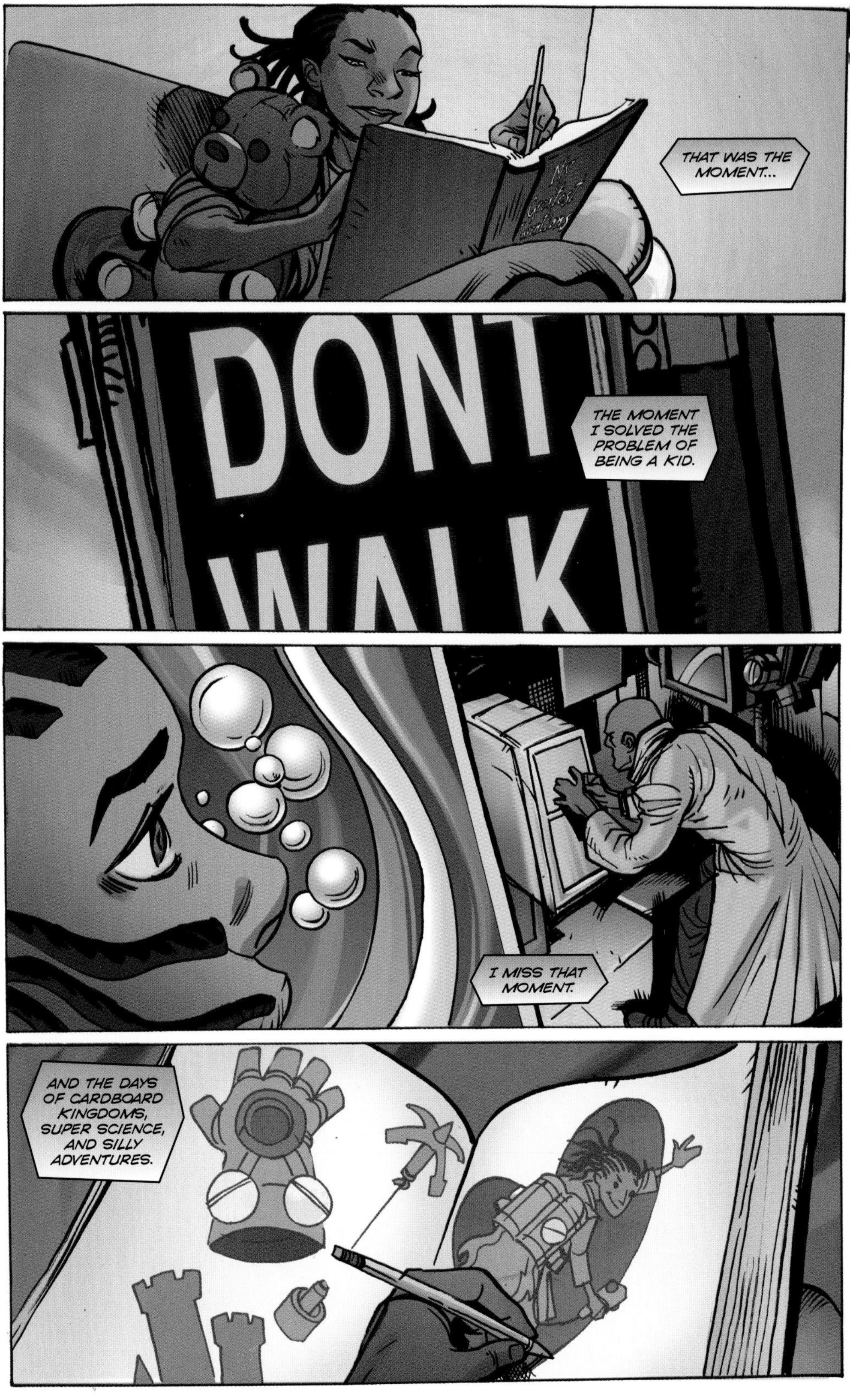
THAT WAS THE MOMENT...
DONT WALK
THE MOMENT I SOLVED THE PROBLEM OF BEING A KID.
I MISS THAT MOMENT.
AND THE DAYS OF CARDBOARD KINGDOMS, SUPER SCIENCE, AND SILLY ADVENTURES.

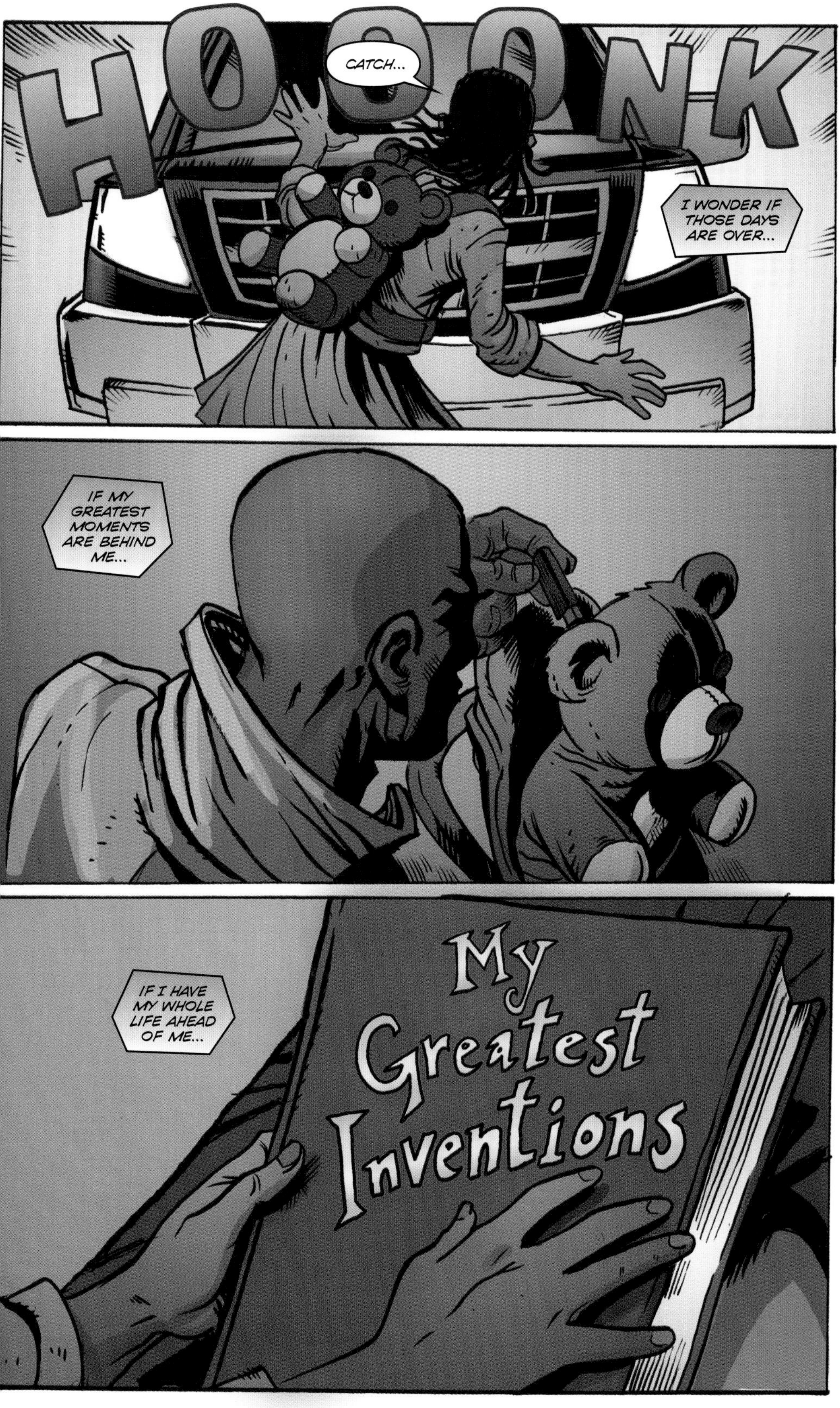
HOOONK
CATCH...
I WONDER IF THOSE DAYS ARE OVER...
IF MY GREATEST MOMENTS ARE BEHIND ME...
IF I HAVE MY WHOLE LIFE AHEAD OF ME...
My Greatest Inventions

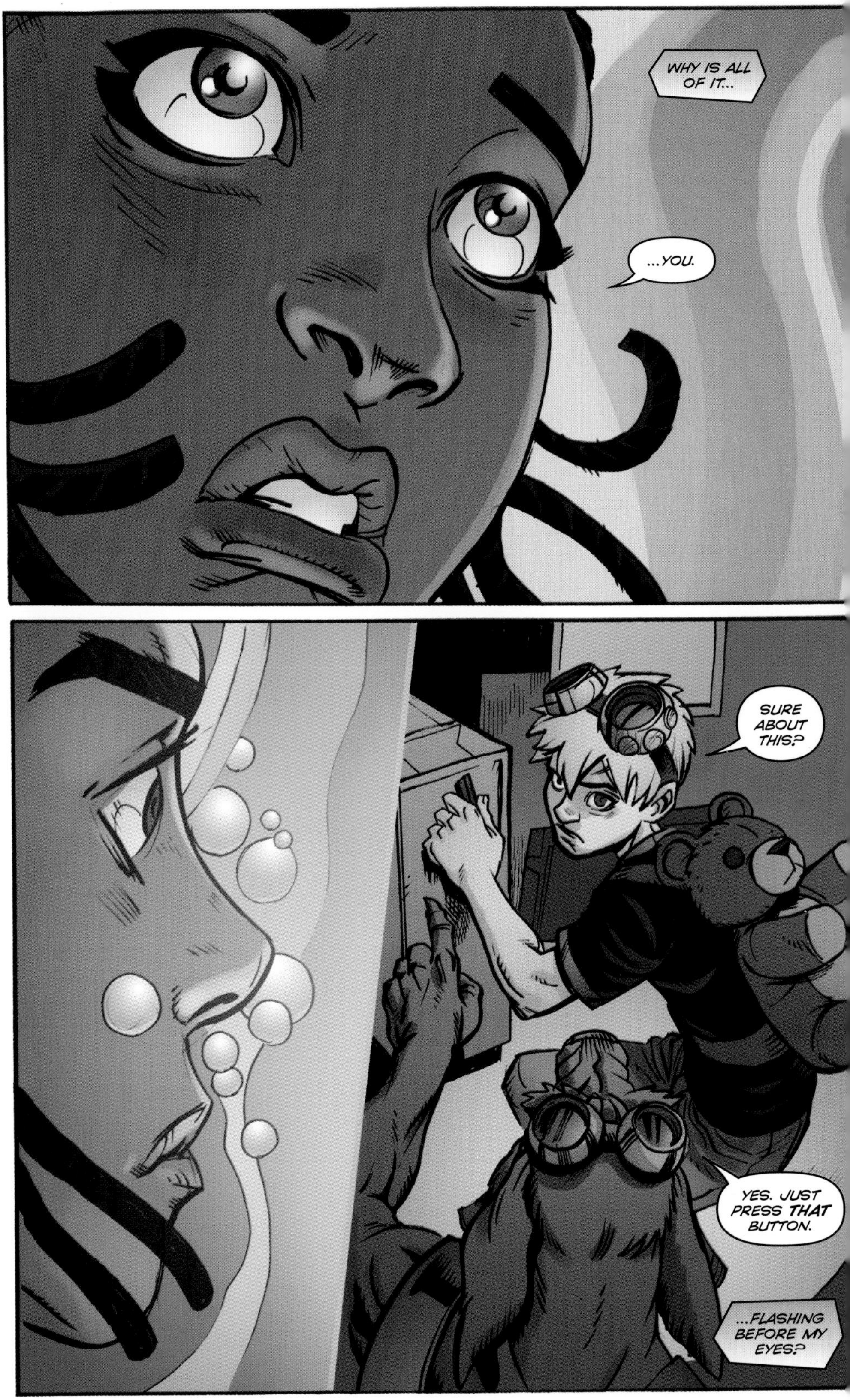
WHY IS ALL OF IT...
...YOU.
SURE ABOUT THIS?
YES. JUST PRESS THAT BUTTON.
...FLASHING BEFORE MY EYES?

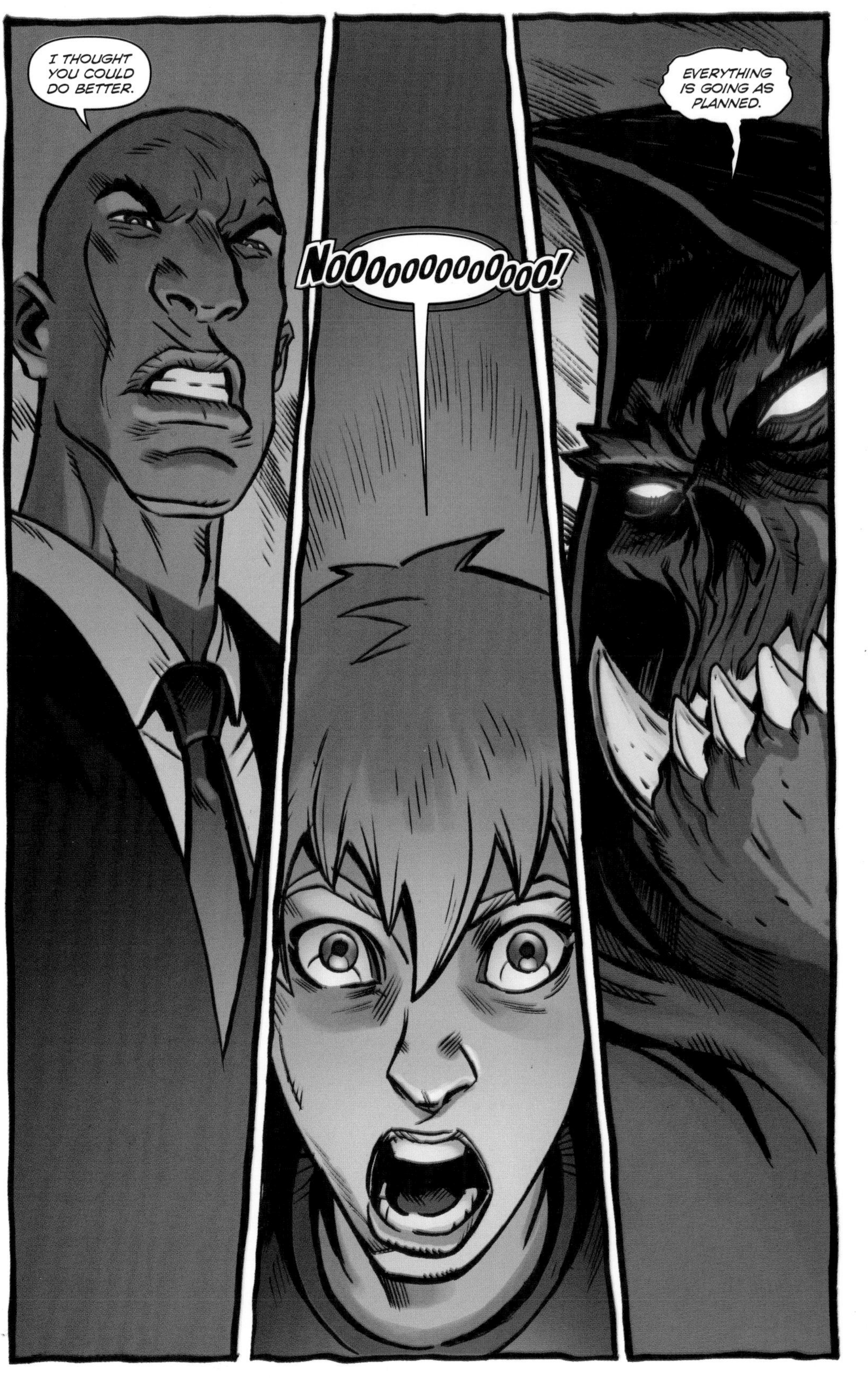
I THOUGHT YOU COULD DO BETTER.
NOOOOOOOOOOOOOO!
EVERYTHING IS GOING AS PLANNED.

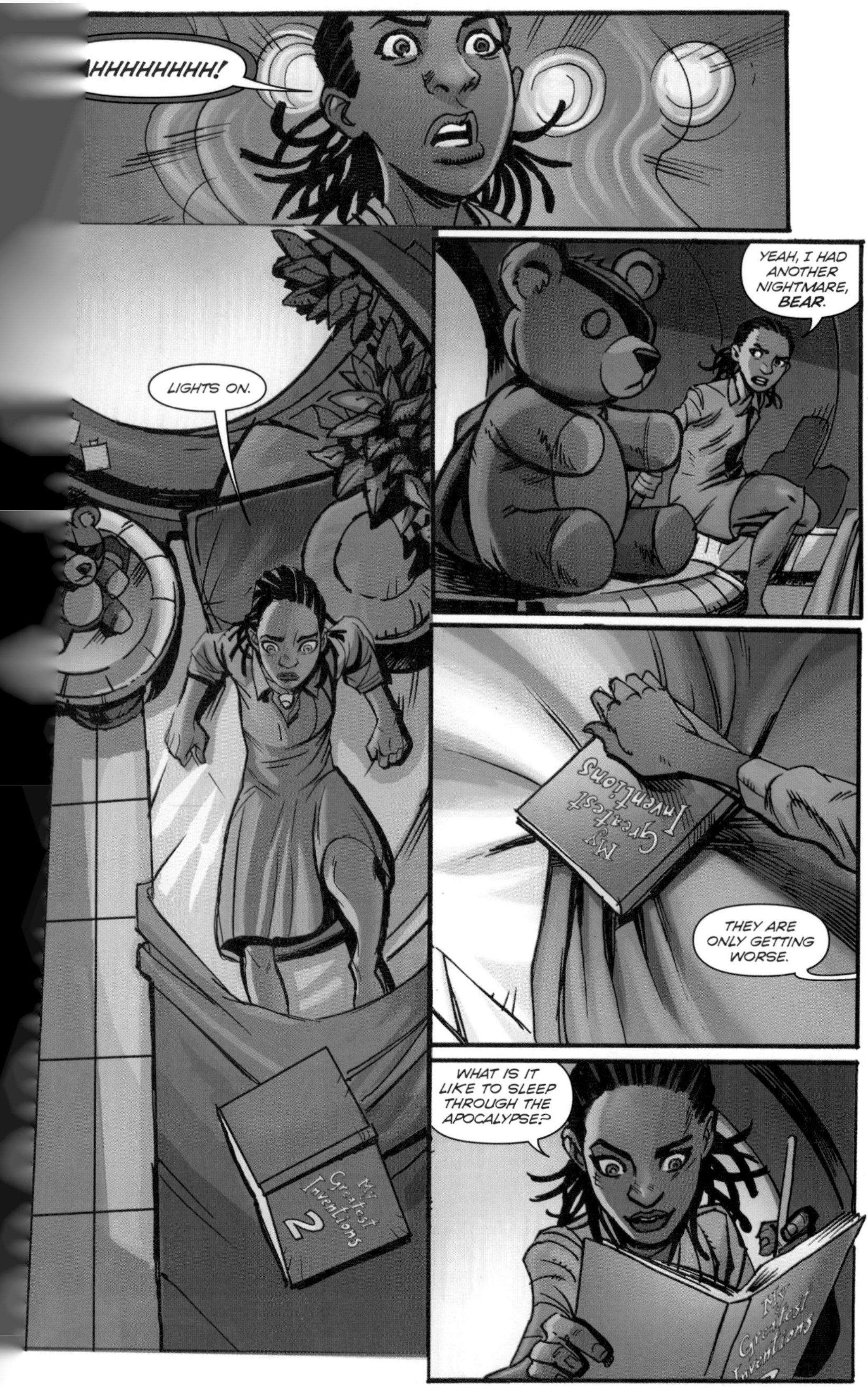
HHHHHHHHH!
LIGHTS ON.
My Greatest Inventions 2
YEAH, I HAD ANOTHER NIGHTMARE, BEAR.
My Greatest Inventions
THEY ARE ONLY GETTING WORSE.
WHAT IS IT LIKE TO SLEEP THROUGH THE APOCALYPSE?
My Greatest Inventions

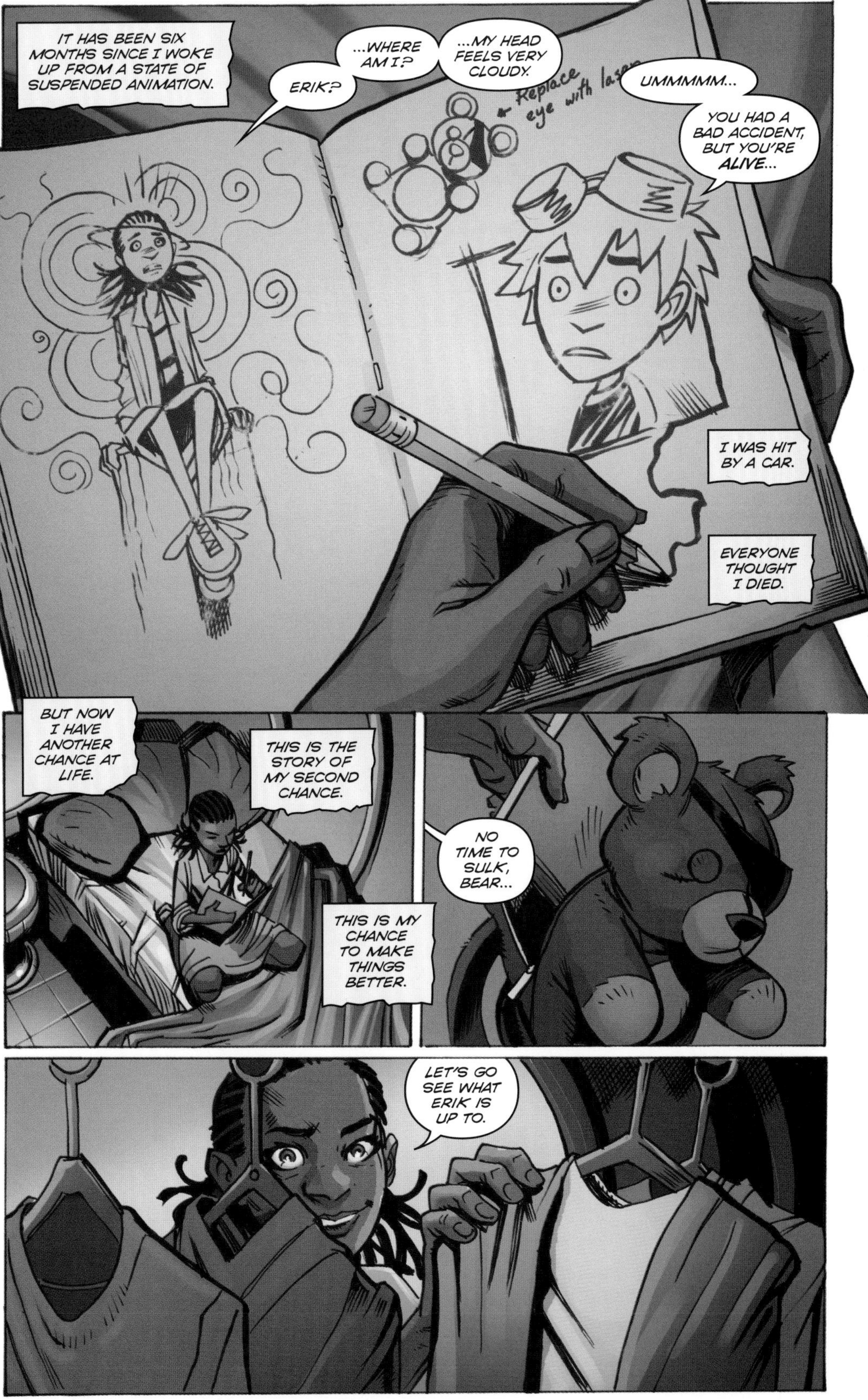
IT HAS BEEN SIX MONTHS SINCE I WOKE UP FROM A STATE OF SUSPENDED ANIMATION.
ERIK?
...WHERE AM I?
...MY HEAD FEELS VERY CLOUDY.
Replace eye with
UMMMMM...
YOU HAD A BAD ACCIDENT, BUT YOU'RE ALIVE...
I WAS HIT BY A CAR.
EVERYONE THOUGHT I DIED.
BUT NOW I HAVE ANOTHER CHANCE AT LIFE.
THIS IS THE STORY OF MY SECOND CHANCE.
THIS IS MY CHANCE TO MAKE THINGS BETTER.
NO TIME TO SULK, BEAR...
LET'S GO SEE WHAT ERIK IS UP TO.

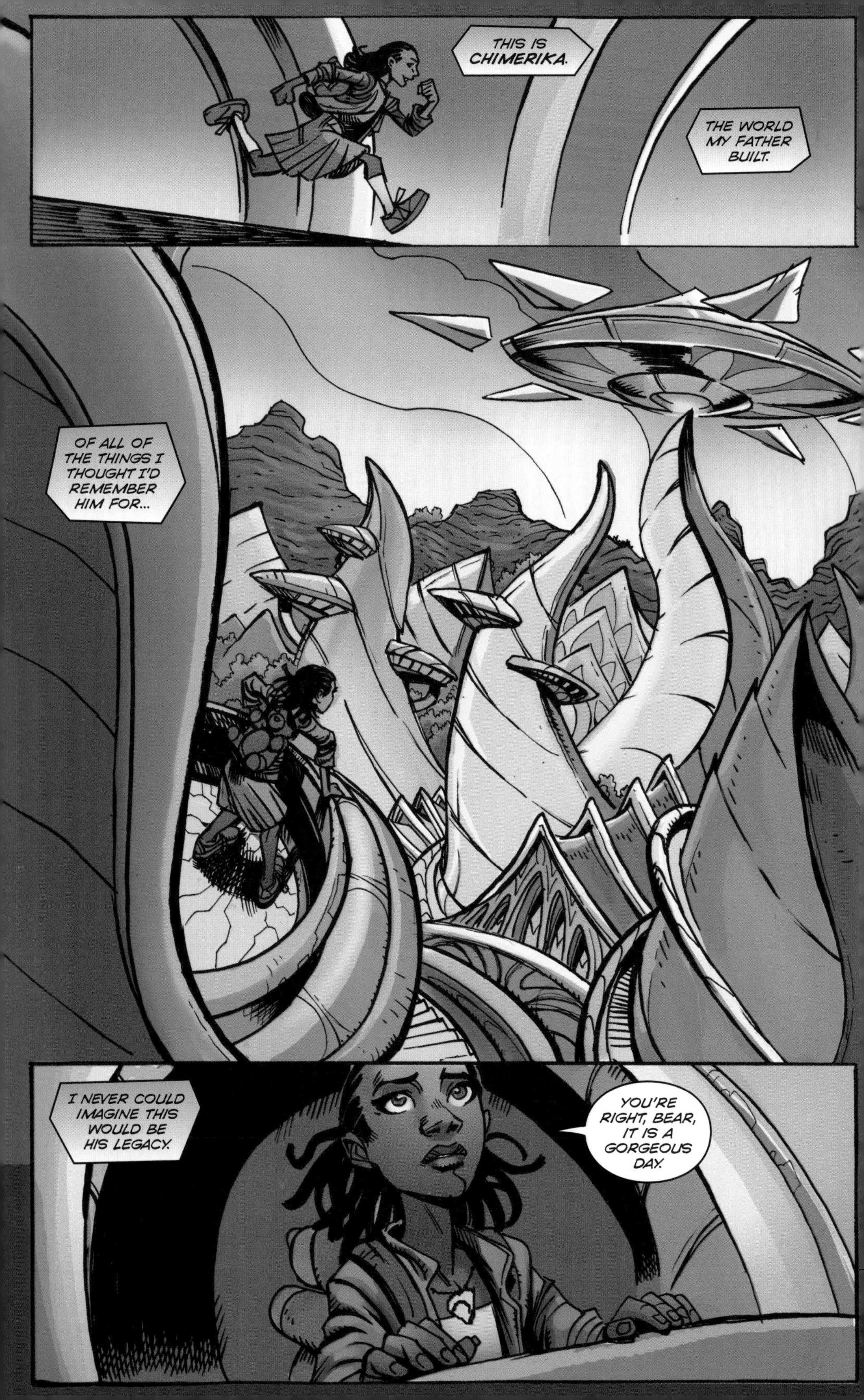
THIS IS CHIMERIKA.
THE WORLD MY FATHER BUILT.
OF ALL OF THE THINGS I THOUGHT I'D REMEMBER HIM FOR...
I NEVER COULD IMAGINE THIS WOULD BE HIS LEGACY.
YOU'RE RIGHT, BEAR, IT IS A GORGEOUS DAY.

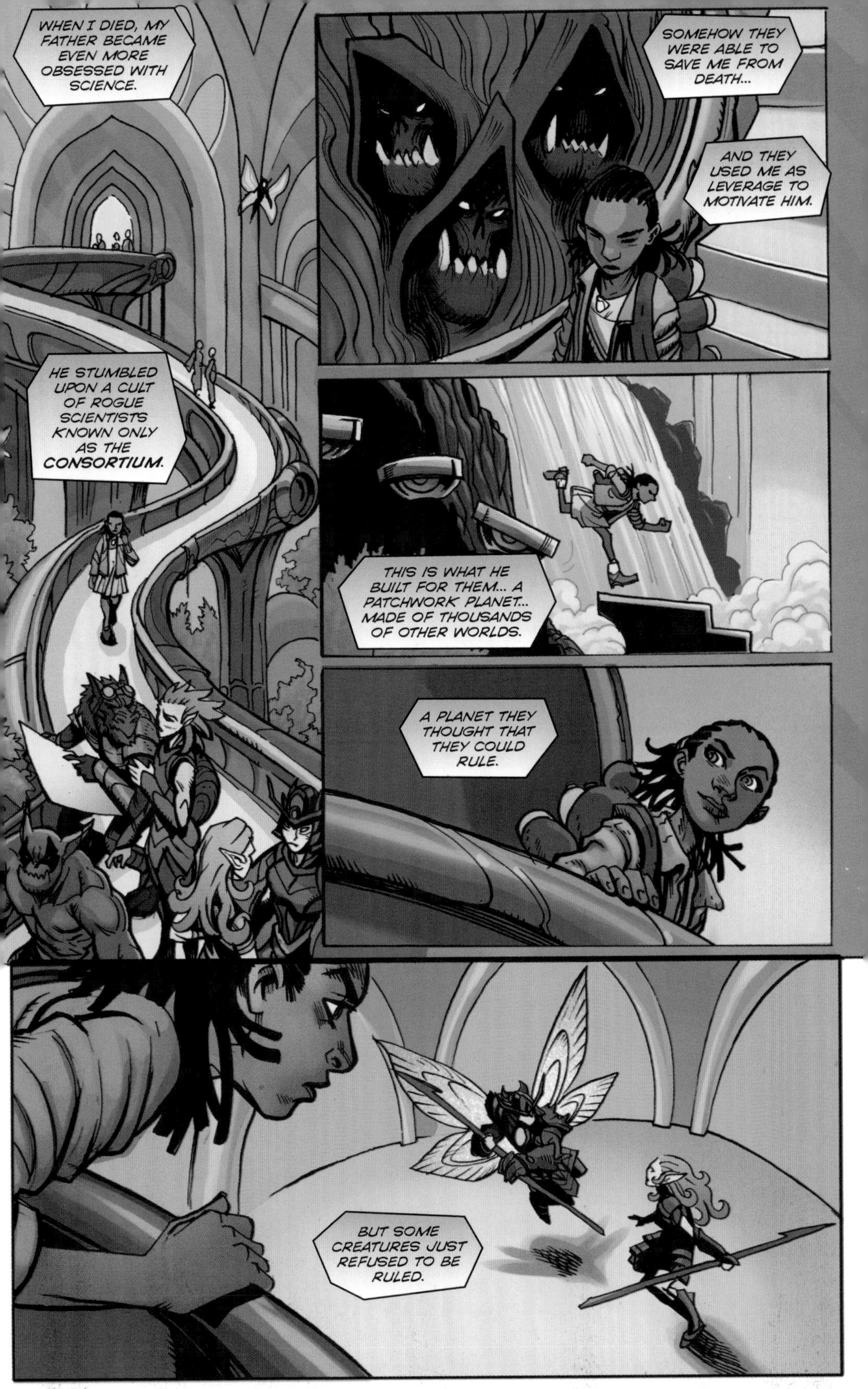
WHEN I DIED, MY FATHER BECAME EVEN MORE OBSESSED WITH SCIENCE.
SOMEHOW THEY WERE ABLE TO SAVE ME FROM DEATH...
AND THEY USED ME AS LEVERAGE TO MOTIVATE HIM.
HE STUMBLED UPON A CULT OF ROGUE SCIENTISTS KNOWN ONLY AS THE CONSORTIUM.
THIS IS WHAT HE BUILT FOR THEM... A PATCHWORK PLANET... MADE OF THOUSANDS OF OTHER WORLDS.
A PLANET THEY THOUGHT THAT THEY COULD RULE.
BUT SOME CREATURES JUST REFUSED TO BE RULED.

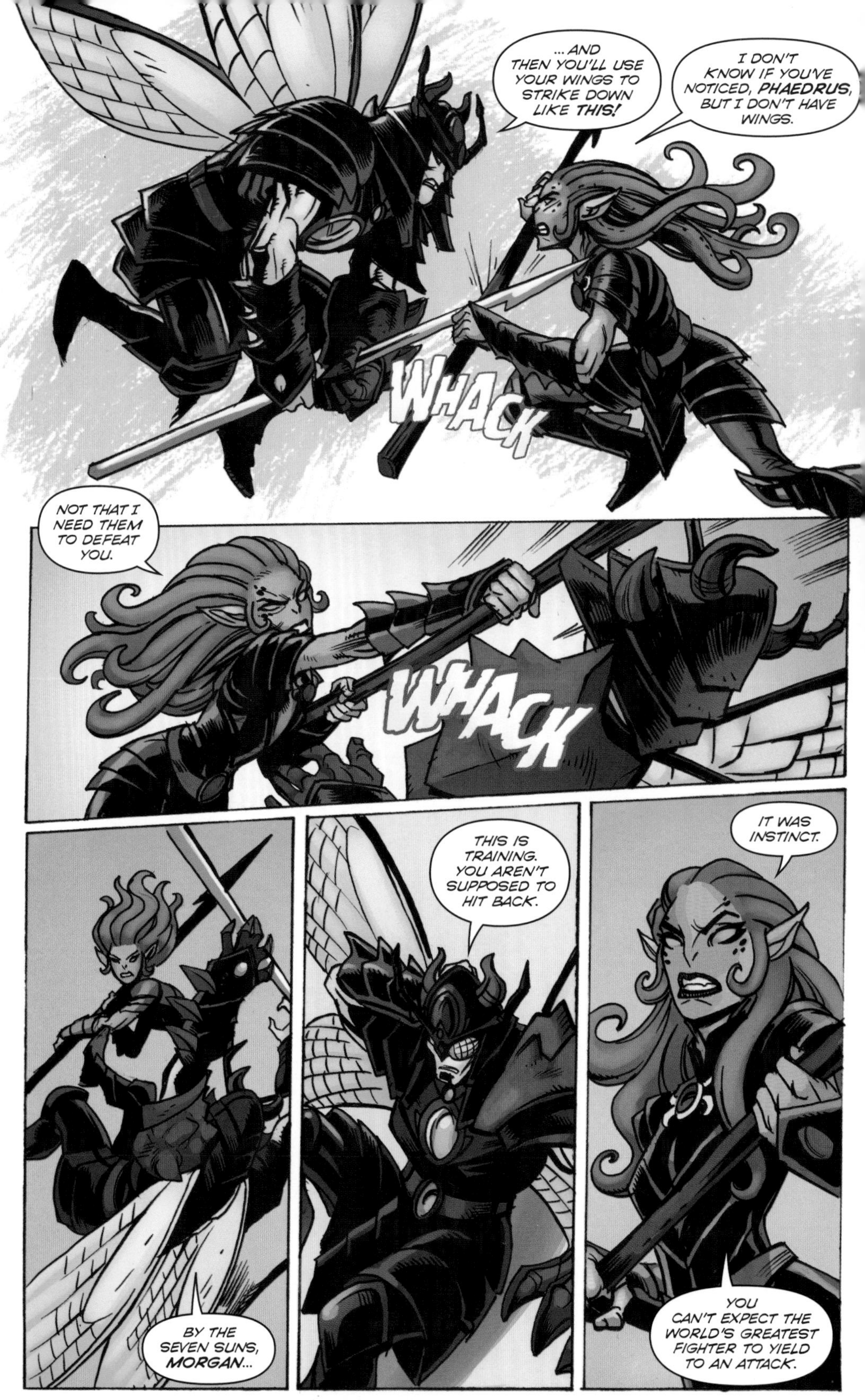
...AND THEN YOU'LL USE YOUR WINGS TO STRIKE DOWN LIKE THIS!
I DON'T KNOW IF YOU'VE NOTICED, PHAEDRUS, BUT I DON'T HAVE WINGS.
WHACK
NOT THAT I NEED THEM TO DEFEAT YOU.
WHACK
BY THE SEVEN SUNS, MORGAN...
THIS IS TRAINING. YOU AREN'T SUPPOSED TO HIT BACK.
IT WAS INSTINCT.
YOU CAN'T EXPECT THE WORLD'S GREATEST FIGHTER TO YIELD TO AN ATTACK.

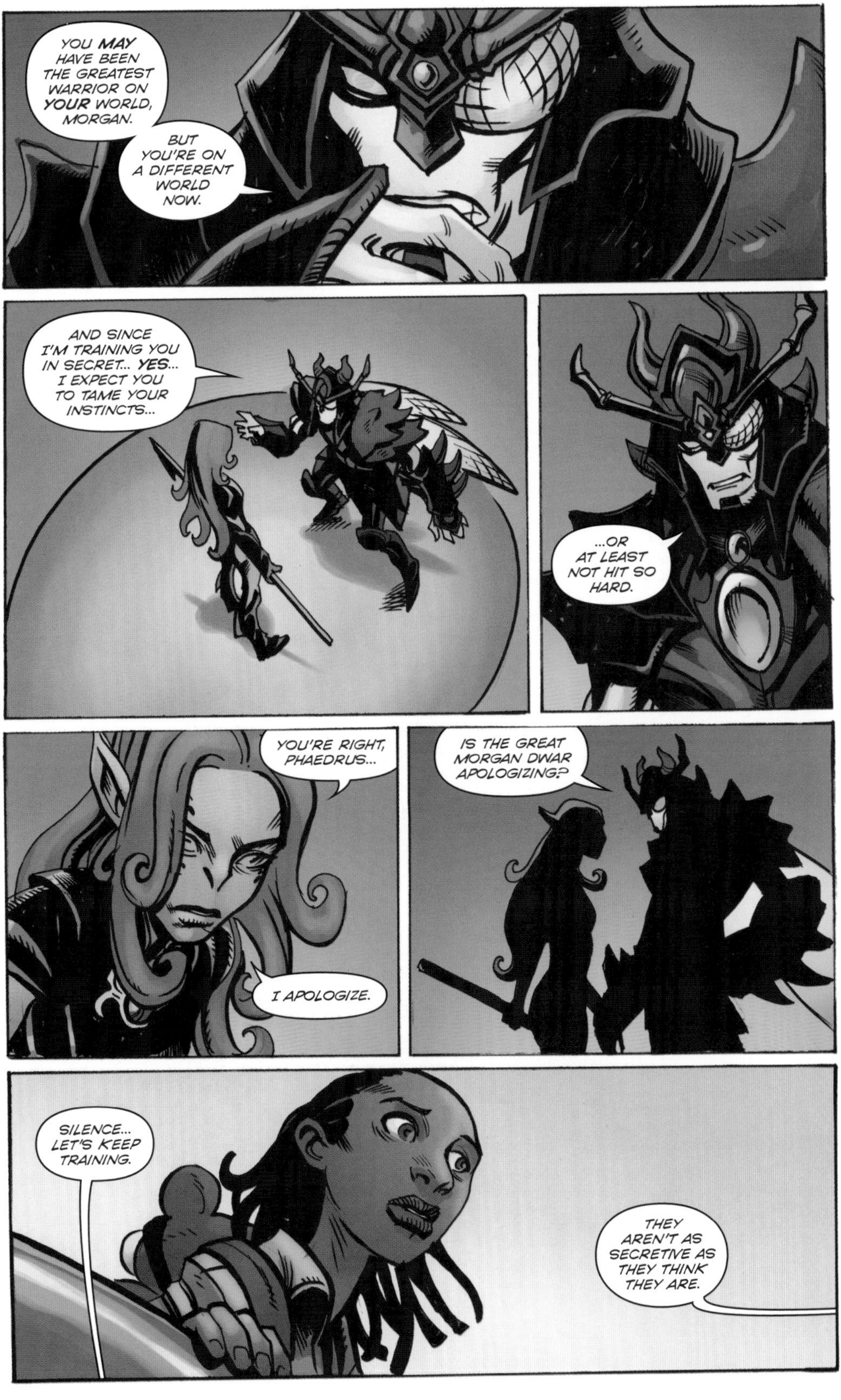
YOU **MAY** HAVE BEEN THE GREATEST WARRIOR ON **YOUR** WORLD, MORGAN.
BUT YOU'RE ON A DIFFERENT WORLD NOW.
AND SINCE I'M TRAINING YOU IN SECRET... **YES**... I EXPECT YOU TO TAME YOUR INSTINCTS...
...OR AT LEAST NOT HIT SO HARD.
YOU'RE RIGHT, PHAEDRUS...
I APOLOGIZE.
IS THE GREAT MORGAN DWAR APOLOGIZING?
SILENCE... LET'S KEEP TRAINING.
THEY AREN'T AS SECRETIVE AS THEY THINK THEY ARE.

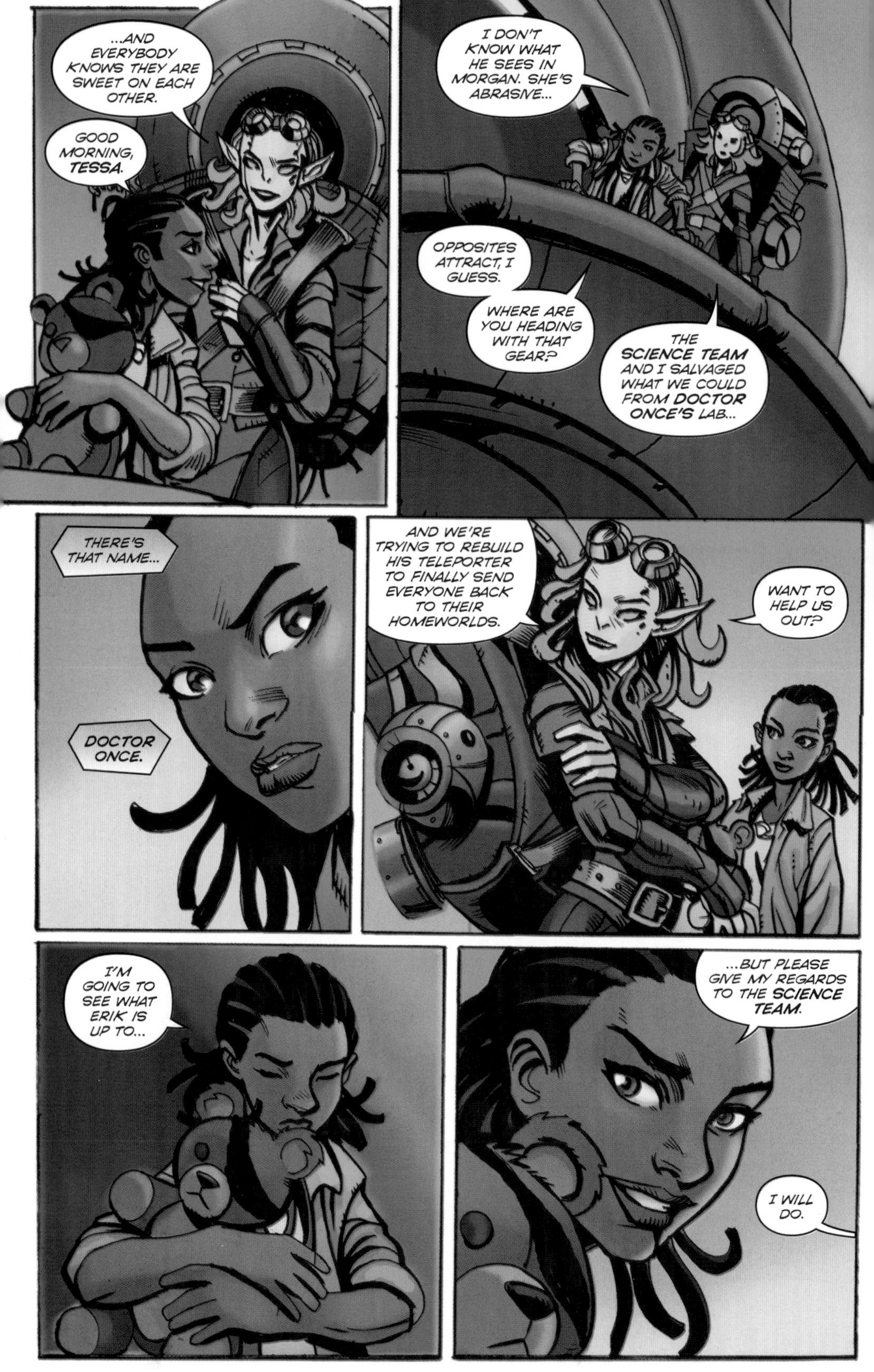

...AND EVERYBODY KNOWS THEY ARE SWEET ON EACH OTHER.
GOOD MORNING, TESSA.
I DON'T KNOW WHAT HE SEES IN MORGAN. SHE'S ABRASIVE...
OPPOSITES ATTRACT, I GUESS.
WHERE ARE YOU HEADING WITH THAT GEAR?
THE SCIENCE TEAM AND I SALVAGED WHAT WE COULD FROM DOCTOR ONCE'S LAB...
THERE'S THAT NAME...
DOCTOR ONCE.
AND WE'RE TRYING TO REBUILD HIS TELEPORTER TO FINALLY SEND EVERYONE BACK TO THEIR HOMEWORLDS.
WANT TO HELP US OUT?
I'M GOING TO SEE WHAT ERIK IS UP TO...
...BUT PLEASE GIVE MY REGARDS TO THE SCIENCE TEAM.
I WILL DO.

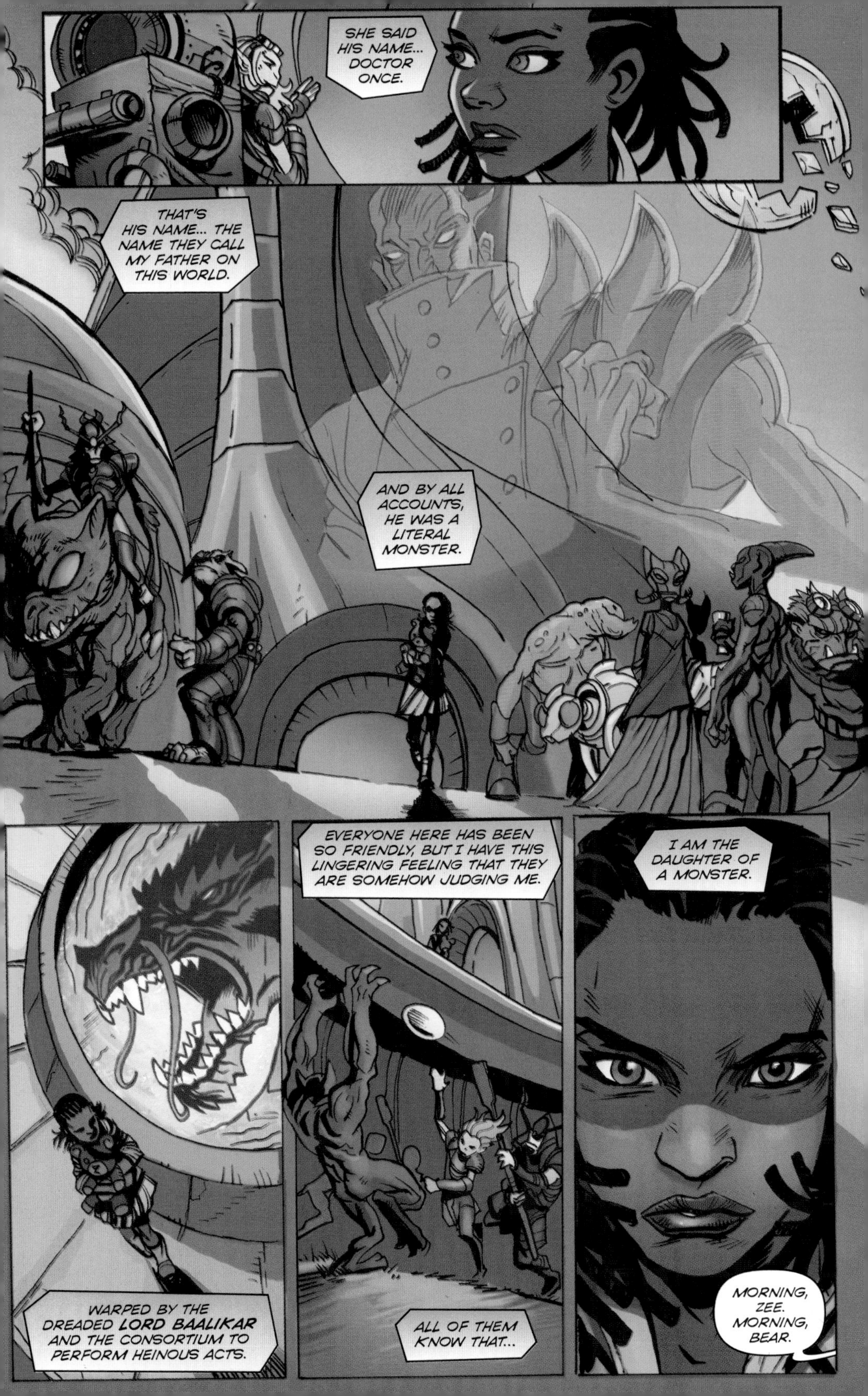
SHE SAID HIS NAME... DOCTOR ONCE.
THAT'S HIS NAME... THE NAME THEY CALL MY FATHER ON THIS WORLD.
AND BY ALL ACCOUNTS, HE WAS A LITERAL MONSTER.
WARPED BY THE DREADED **LORD BAALIKAR** AND THE CONSORTIUM TO PERFORM HEINOUS ACTS.
EVERYONE HERE HAS BEEN SO FRIENDLY, BUT I HAVE THIS LINGERING FEELING THAT THEY ARE SOMEHOW JUDGING ME.
ALL OF THEM KNOW THAT...
I AM THE DAUGHTER OF A MONSTER.
MORNING, ZEE. MORNING, BEAR.

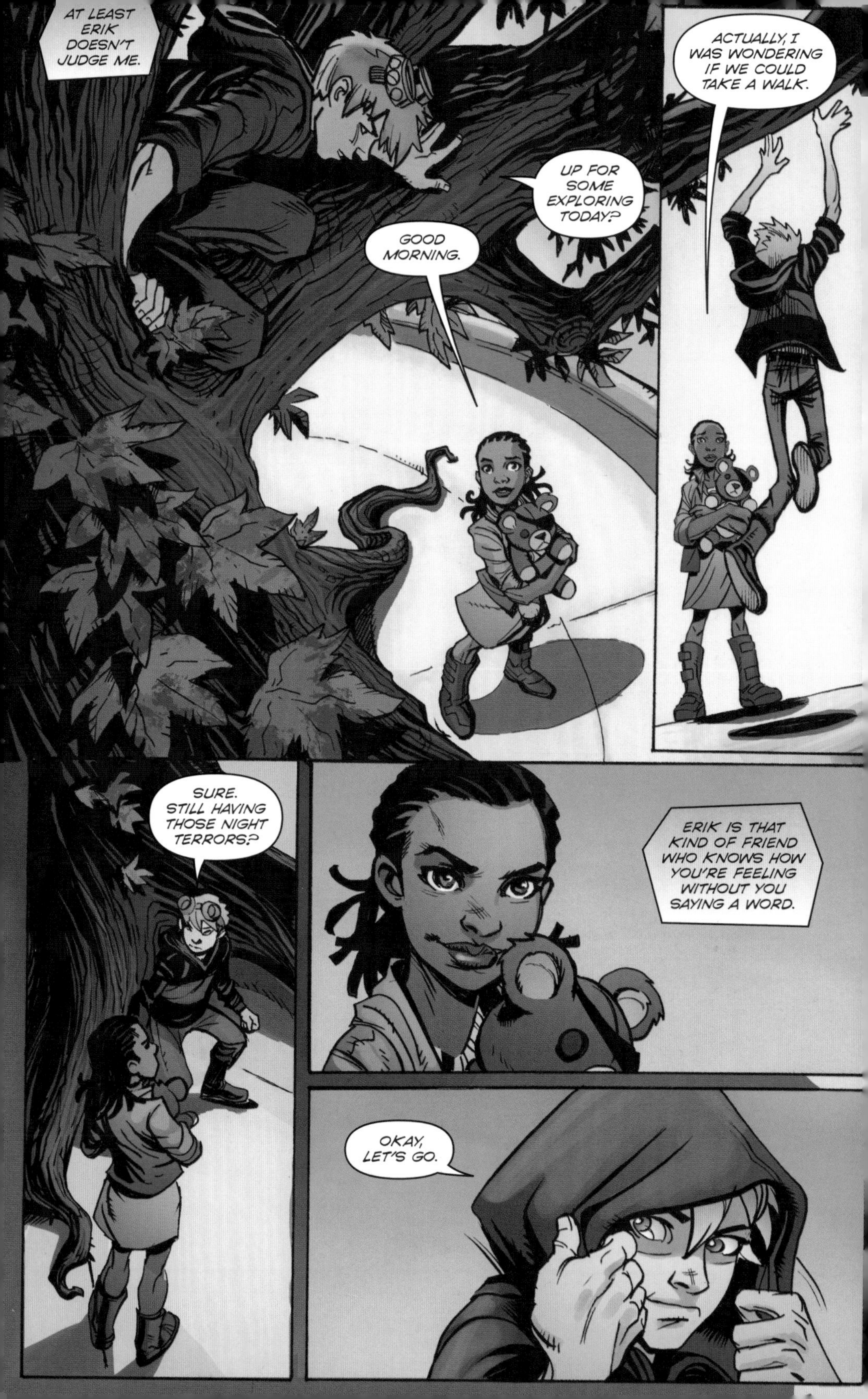

AT LEAST ERIK DOESN'T JUDGE ME.
GOOD MORNING.
UP FOR SOME EXPLORING TODAY?
ACTUALLY, I WAS WONDERING IF WE COULD TAKE A WALK.
SURE. STILL HAVING THOSE NIGHT TERRORS?
ERIK IS THAT KIND OF FRIEND WHO KNOWS HOW YOU'RE FEELING WITHOUT YOU SAYING A WORD.
OKAY, LET'S GO.

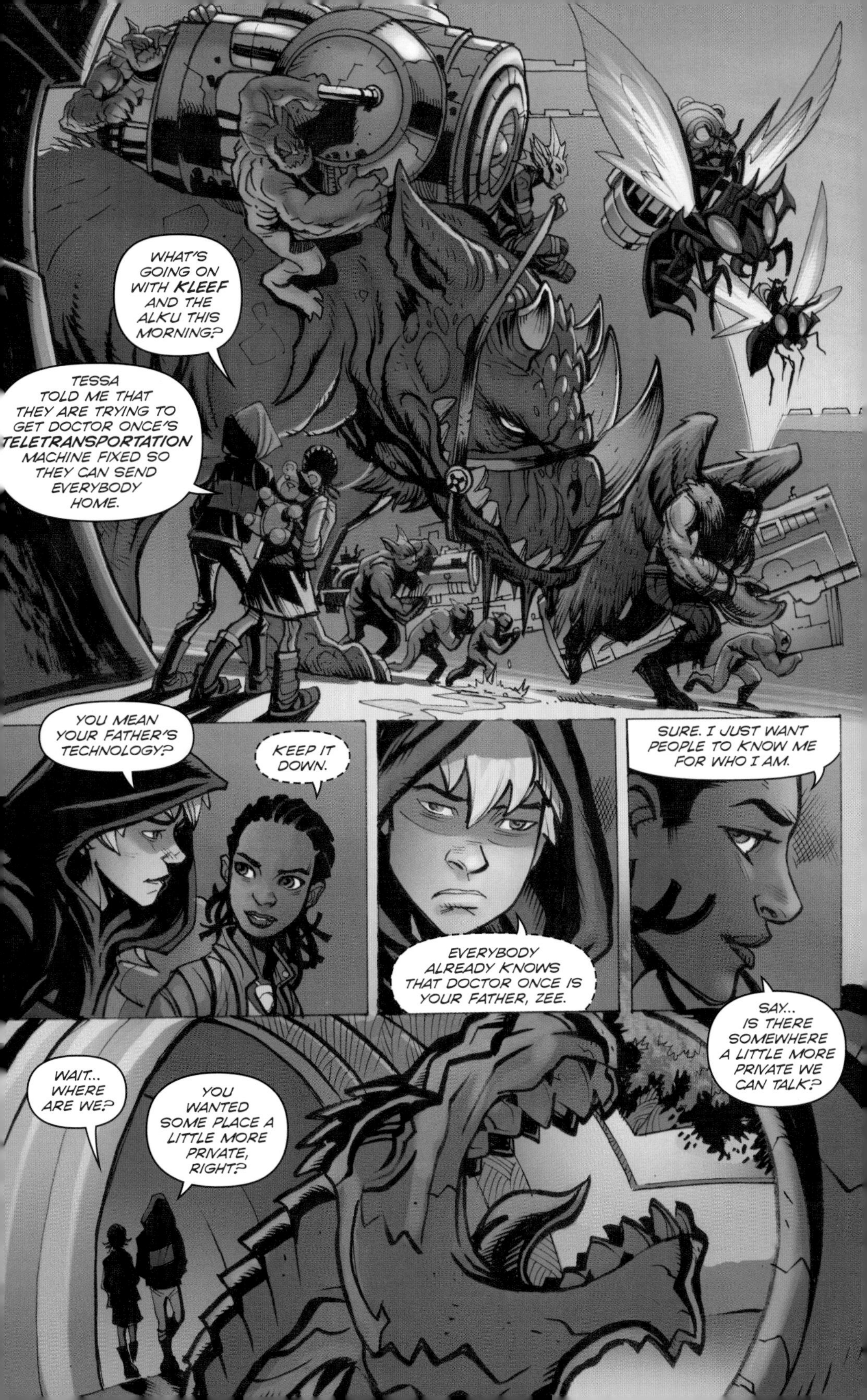
WHAT'S GOING ON WITH KLEEF AND THE ALKU THIS MORNING?
TESSA TOLD ME THAT THEY ARE TRYING TO GET DOCTOR ONCE'S TELETRANSPORTATION MACHINE FIXED SO THEY CAN SEND EVERYBODY HOME.
YOU MEAN YOUR FATHER'S TECHNOLOGY?
KEEP IT DOWN.
EVERYBODY ALREADY KNOWS THAT DOCTOR ONCE IS YOUR FATHER, ZEE.
SURE. I JUST WANT PEOPLE TO KNOW ME FOR WHO I AM.
SAY... IS THERE SOMEWHERE A LITTLE MORE PRIVATE WE CAN TALK?
WAIT... WHERE ARE WE?
YOU WANTED SOME PLACE A LITTLE MORE PRIVATE, RIGHT?

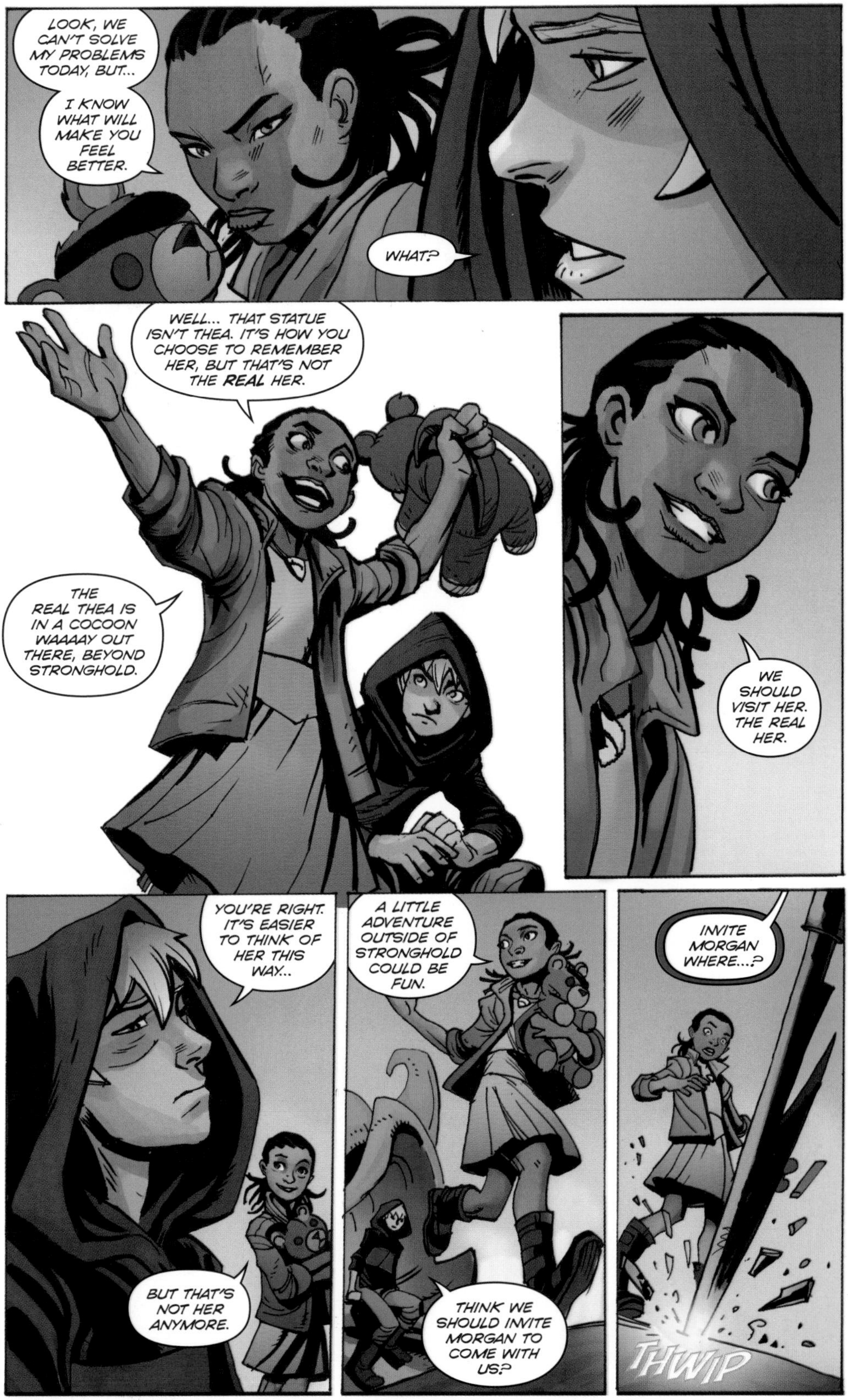
LOOK, WE CAN'T SOLVE MY PROBLEMS TODAY, BUT...
I KNOW WHAT WILL MAKE YOU FEEL BETTER.
WHAT?
WELL... THAT STATUE ISN'T THEA. IT'S HOW YOU CHOOSE TO REMEMBER HER, BUT THAT'S NOT THE REAL HER.
THE REAL THEA IS IN A COCOON WAAAAY OUT THERE, BEYOND STRONGHOLD.
WE SHOULD VISIT HER. THE REAL HER.
YOU'RE RIGHT. IT'S EASIER TO THINK OF HER THIS WAY...
BUT THAT'S NOT HER ANYMORE.
A LITTLE ADVENTURE OUTSIDE OF STRONGHOLD COULD BE FUN.
THINK WE SHOULD INVITE MORGAN TO COME WITH US?
INVITE MORGAN WHERE...?
THWIP

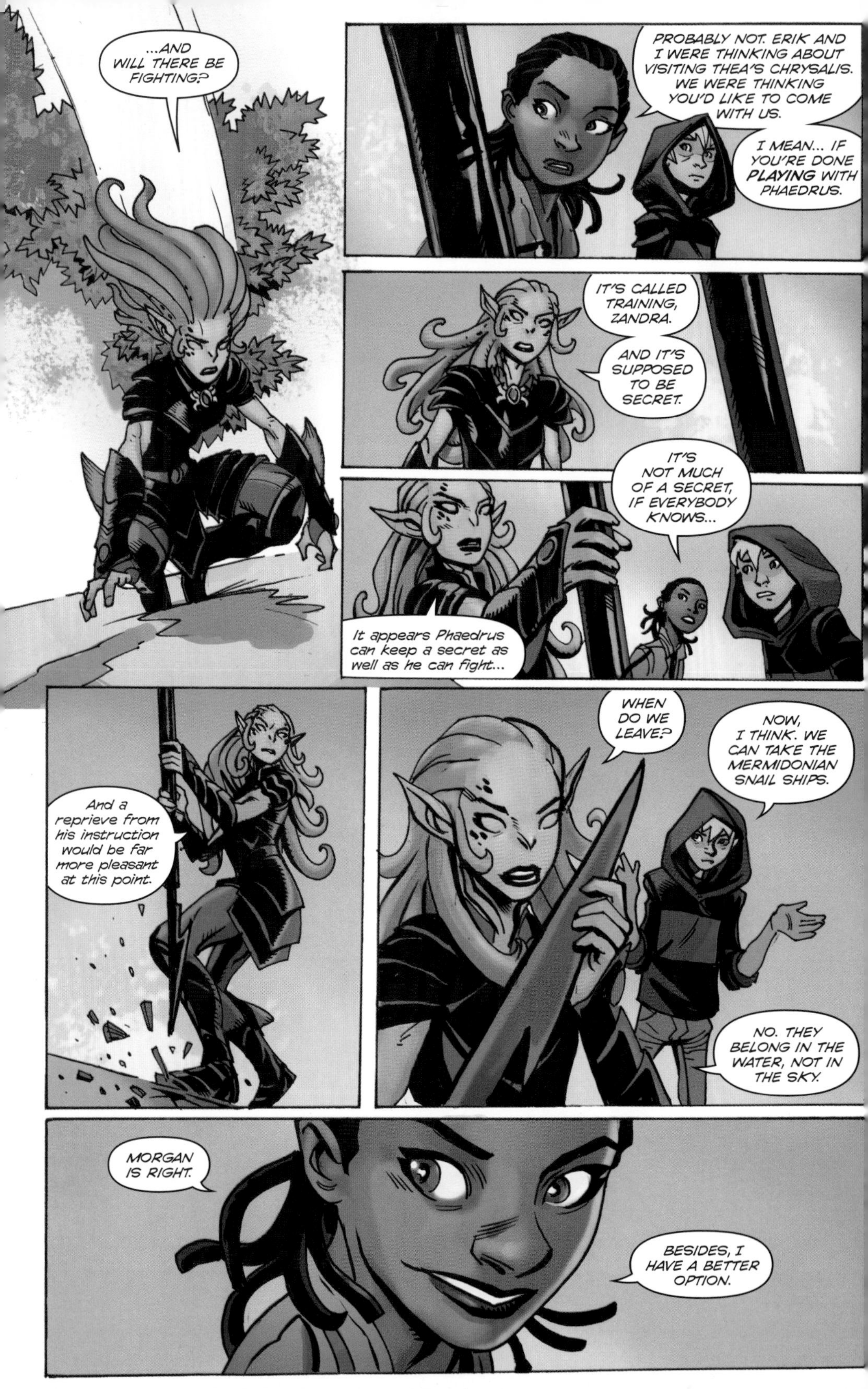
...AND WILL THERE BE FIGHTING?
PROBABLY NOT. ERIK AND I WERE THINKING ABOUT VISITING THEA'S CHRYSALIS. WE WERE THINKING YOU'D LIKE TO COME WITH US.
I MEAN... IF YOU'RE DONE **PLAYING** WITH PHAEDRUS.
IT'S CALLED TRAINING, ZANDRA.
AND IT'S SUPPOSED TO BE SECRET.
IT'S NOT MUCH OF A SECRET, IF EVERYBODY KNOWS...
It appears Phaedrus can keep a secret as well as he can fight...
And a reprieve from his instruction would be far more pleasant at this point.
WHEN DO WE LEAVE?
NOW, I THINK. WE CAN TAKE THE MERMIDONIAN SNAIL SHIPS.
NO. THEY BELONG IN THE WATER, NOT IN THE SKY.
MORGAN IS RIGHT.
BESIDES, I HAVE A BETTER OPTION.

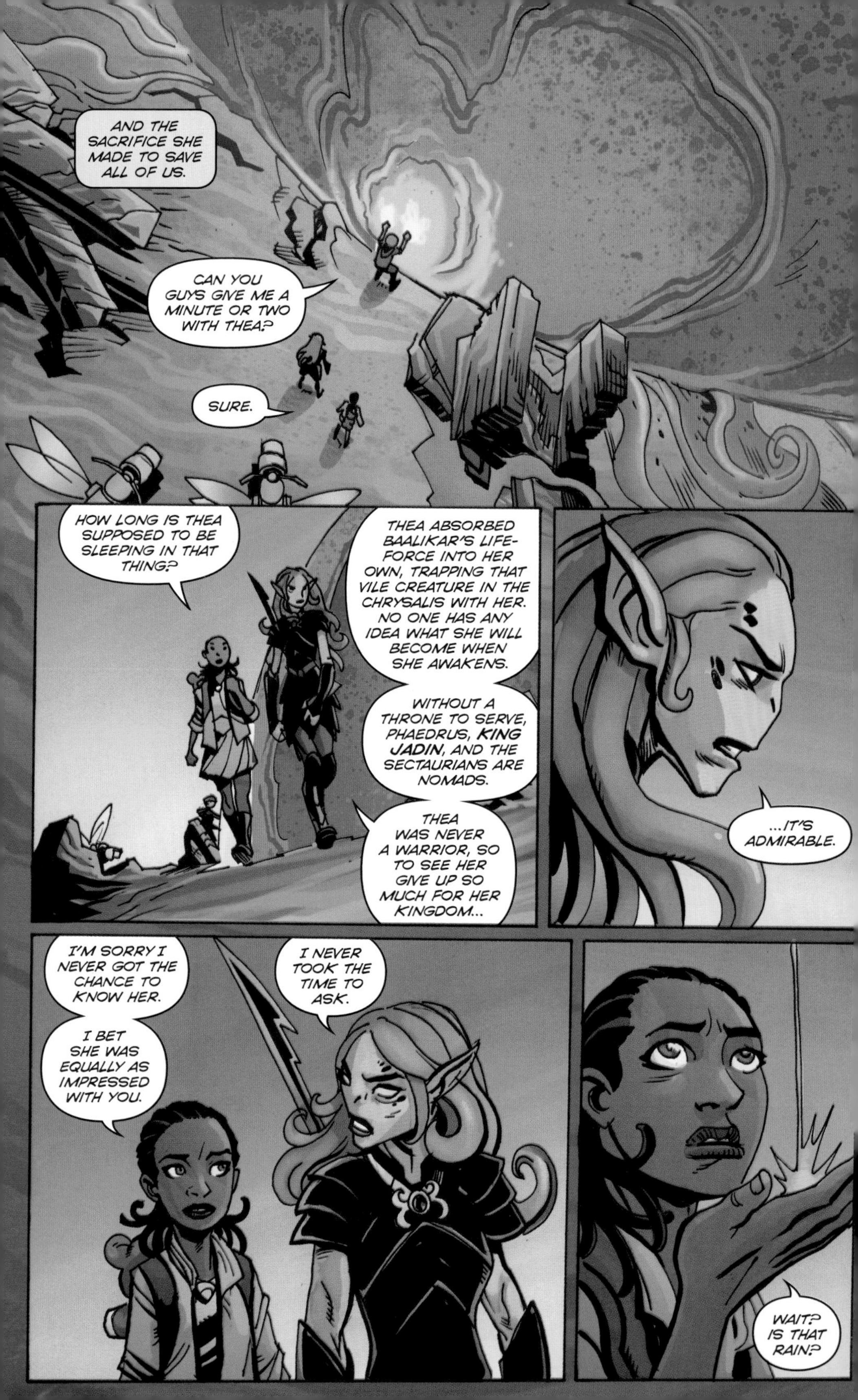
AND THE SACRIFICE SHE MADE TO SAVE ALL OF US.
CAN YOU GUYS GIVE ME A MINUTE OR TWO WITH THEA?
SURE.
HOW LONG IS THEA SUPPOSED TO BE SLEEPING IN THAT THING?
THEA ABSORBED BAALIKAR'S LIFE-FORCE INTO HER OWN, TRAPPING THAT VILE CREATURE IN THE CHRYSALIS WITH HER. NO ONE HAS ANY IDEA WHAT SHE WILL BECOME WHEN SHE AWAKENS.
WITHOUT A THRONE TO SERVE, PHAEDRUS, KING JADIN, AND THE SECTAURIANS ARE NOMADS.
THEA WAS NEVER A WARRIOR, SO TO SEE HER GIVE UP SO MUCH FOR HER KINGDOM...
...IT'S ADMIRABLE.
I'M SORRY I NEVER GOT THE CHANCE TO KNOW HER.
I BET SHE WAS EQUALLY AS IMPRESSED WITH YOU.
I NEVER TOOK THE TIME TO ASK.
WAIT? IS THAT RAIN?

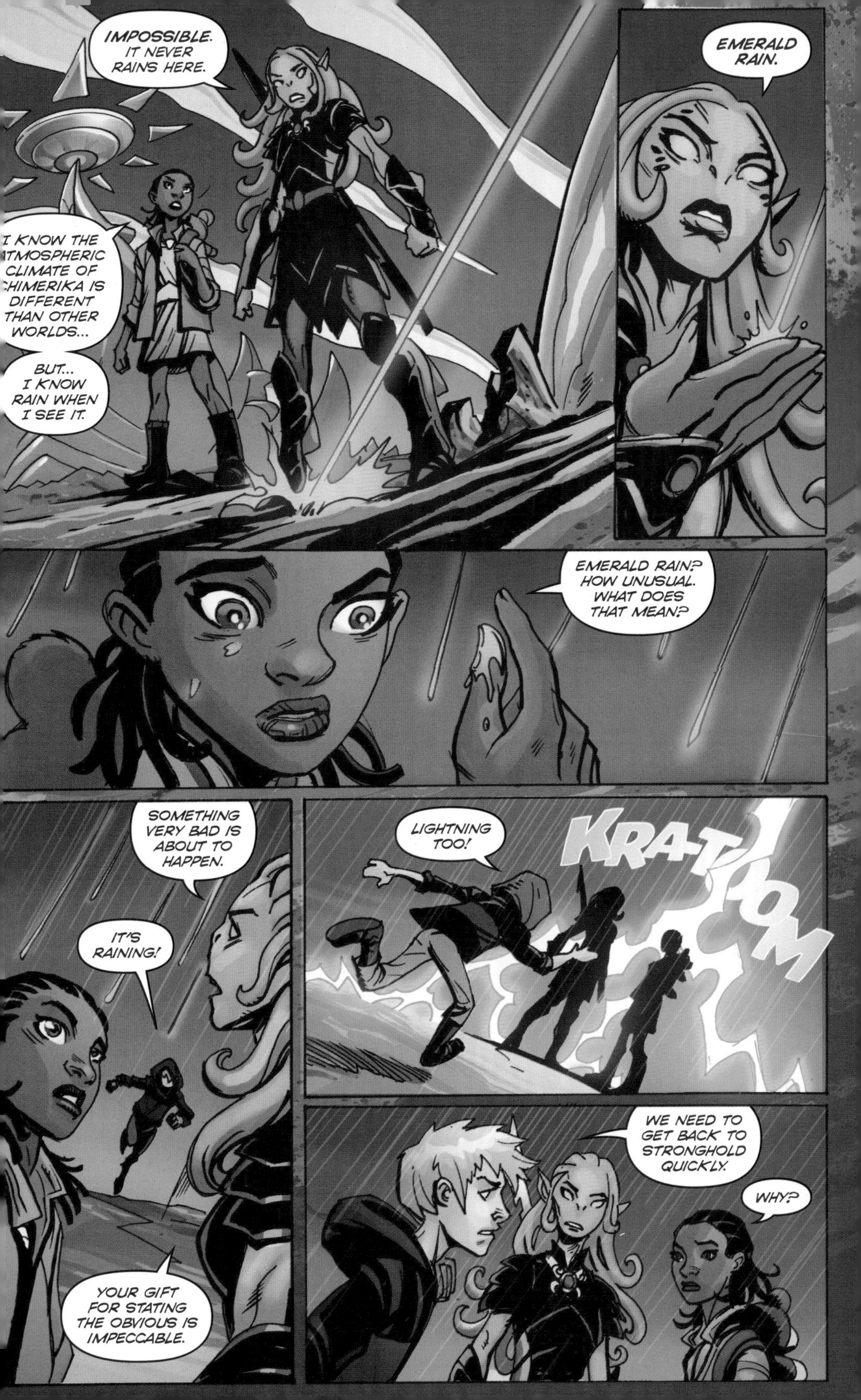
IMPOSSIBLE. IT NEVER RAINS HERE.
I KNOW THE ATMOSPHERIC CLIMATE OF CHIMERIKA IS DIFFERENT THAN OTHER WORLDS...
BUT... I KNOW RAIN WHEN I SEE IT.
EMERALD RAIN.
EMERALD RAIN? HOW UNUSUAL. WHAT DOES THAT MEAN?
SOMETHING VERY BAD IS ABOUT TO HAPPEN.
IT'S RAINING!
YOUR GIFT FOR STATING THE OBVIOUS IS IMPECCABLE.
LIGHTNING TOO!
KRAT-TOOM
WE NEED TO GET BACK TO STRONGHOLD QUICKLY.
WHY?

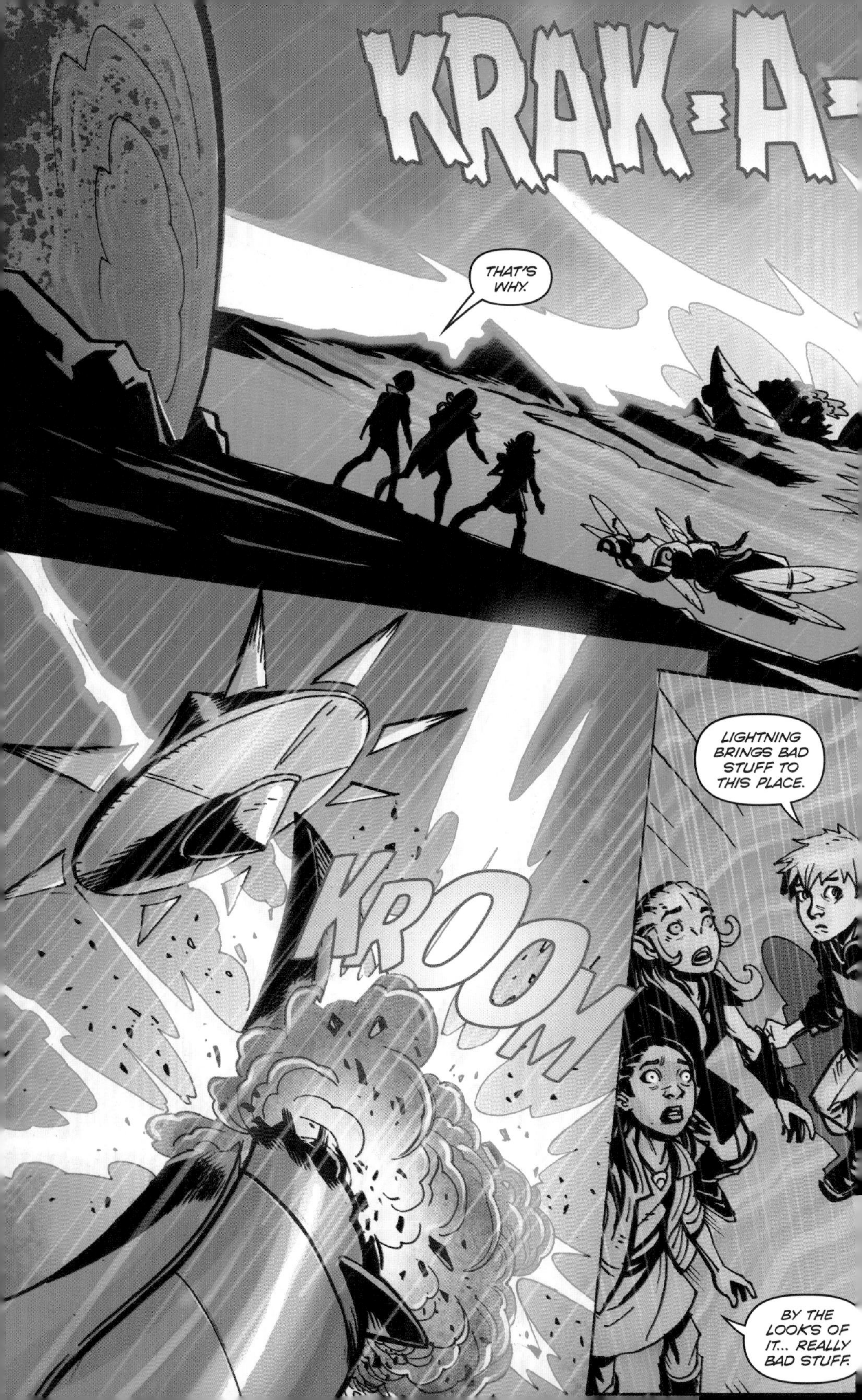
KRAK-A-
THAT'S WHY.
LIGHTNING BRINGS BAD STUFF TO THIS PLACE.
KROOM
BY THE LOOKS OF IT... REALLY BAD STUFF.

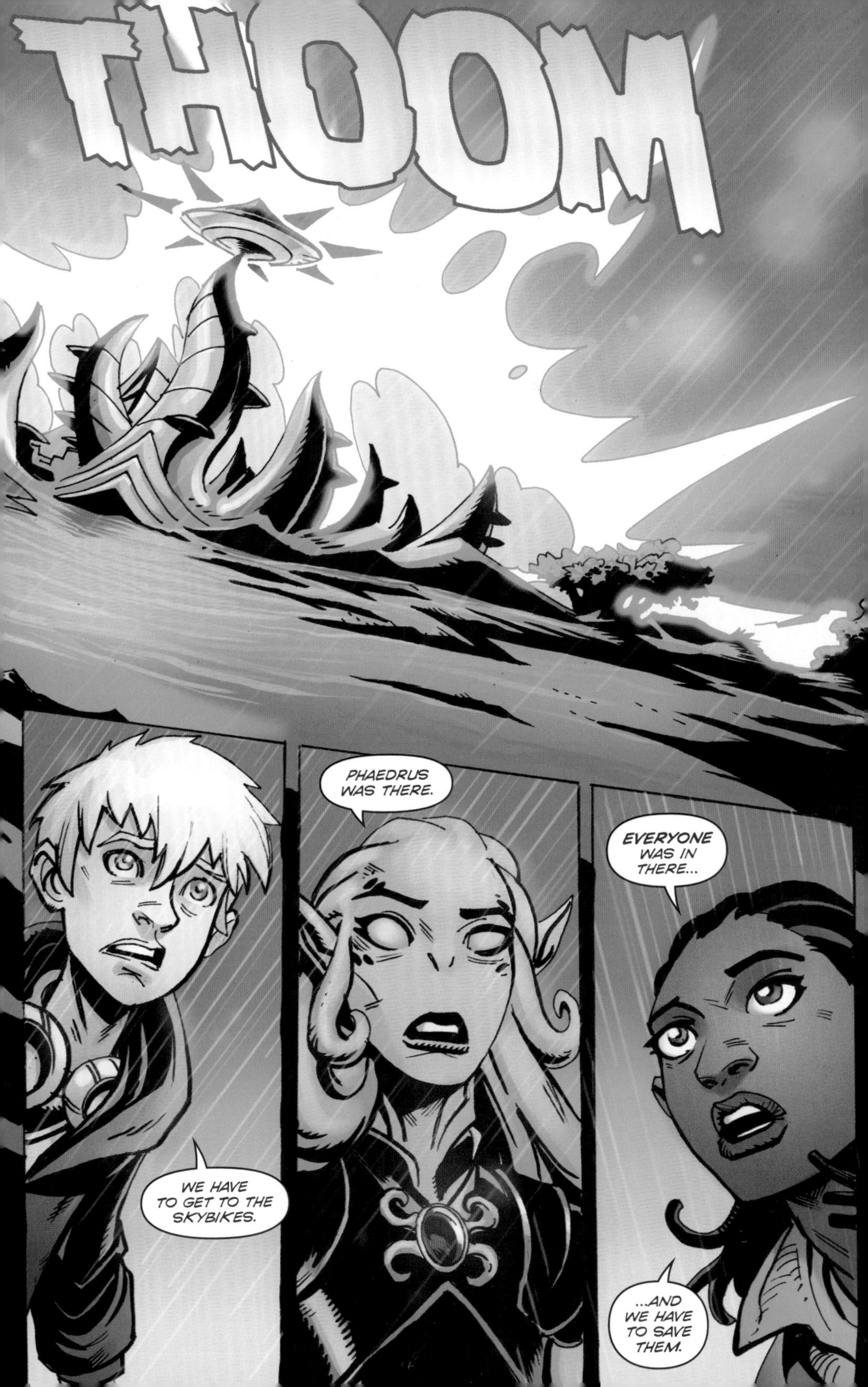
THOOM
WE HAVE TO GET TO THE SKYBIKES.
PHAEDRUS WAS THERE.
EVERYONE WAS IN THERE...
...AND WE HAVE TO SAVE THEM.

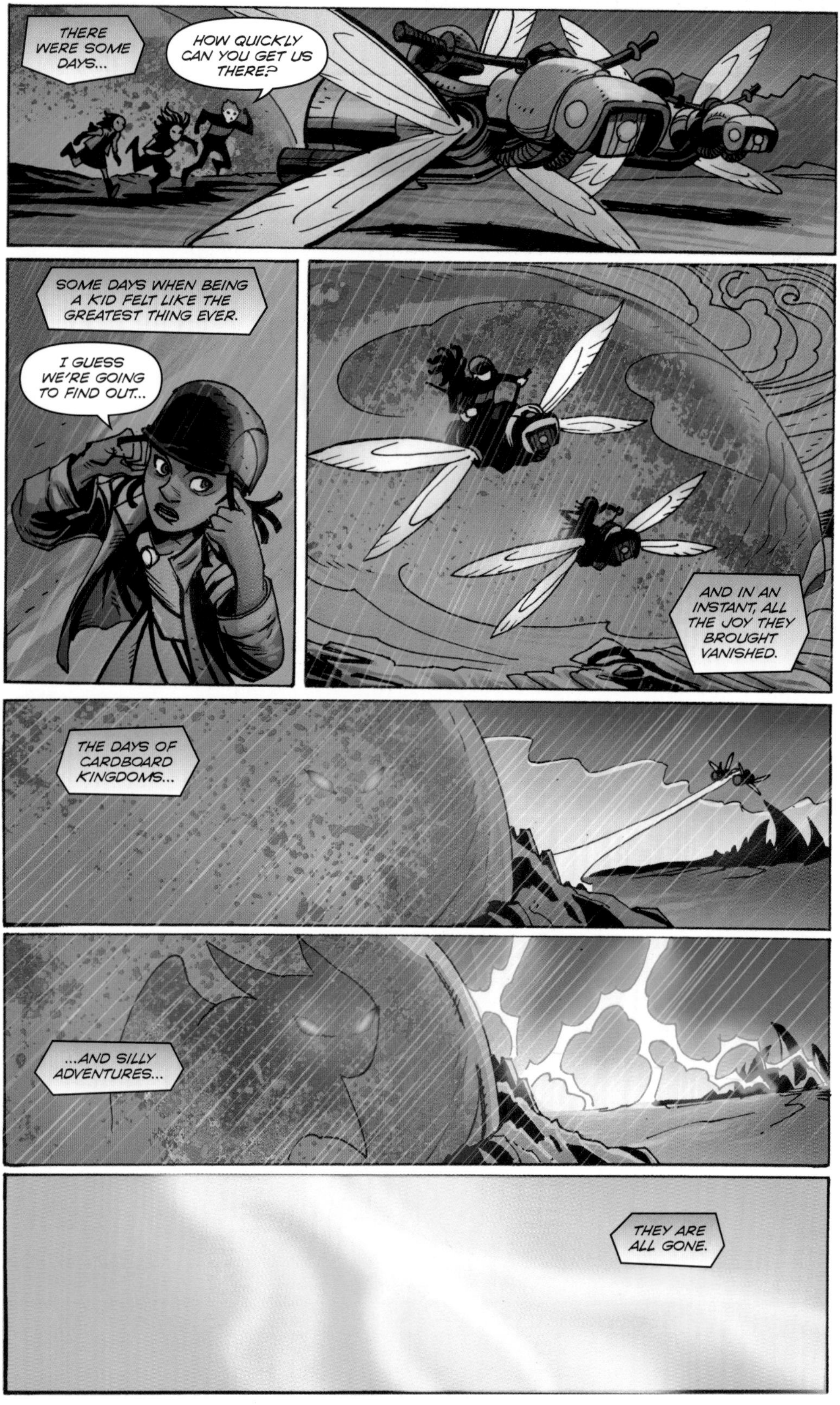
THERE WERE SOME DAYS...
HOW QUICKLY CAN YOU GET US THERE?
SOME DAYS WHEN BEING A KID FELT LIKE THE GREATEST THING EVER.
I GUESS WE'RE GOING TO FIND OUT...
AND IN AN INSTANT, ALL THE JOY THEY BROUGHT VANISHED.
THE DAYS OF CARDBOARD KINGDOMS...
...AND SILLY ADVENTURES...
THEY ARE ALL GONE.

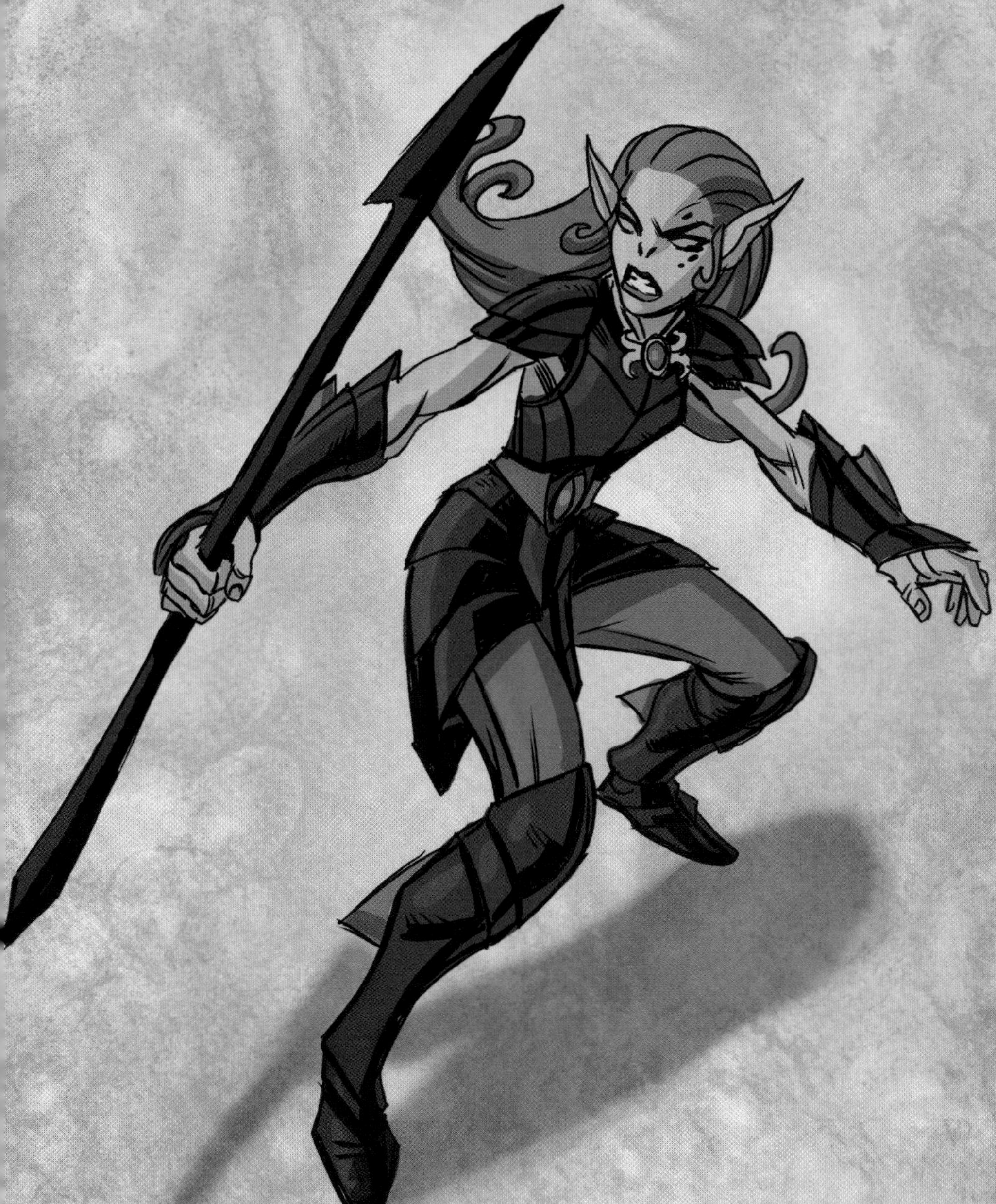

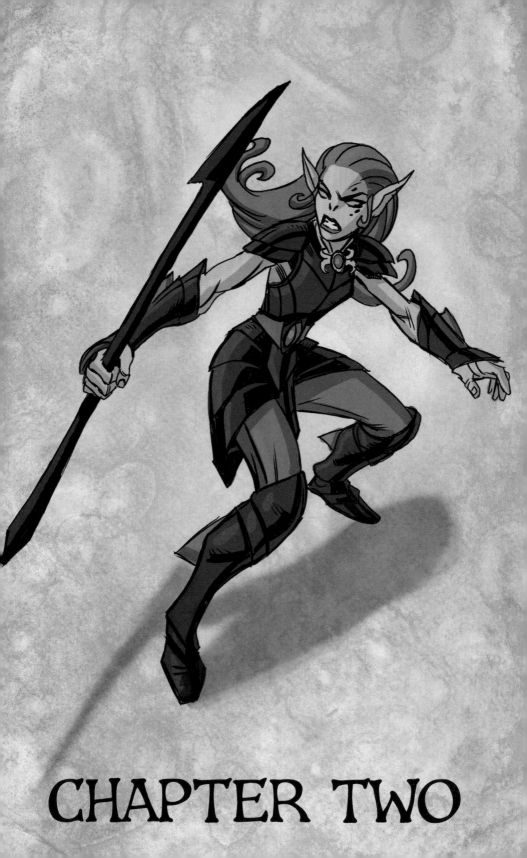

CHAPTER TWO

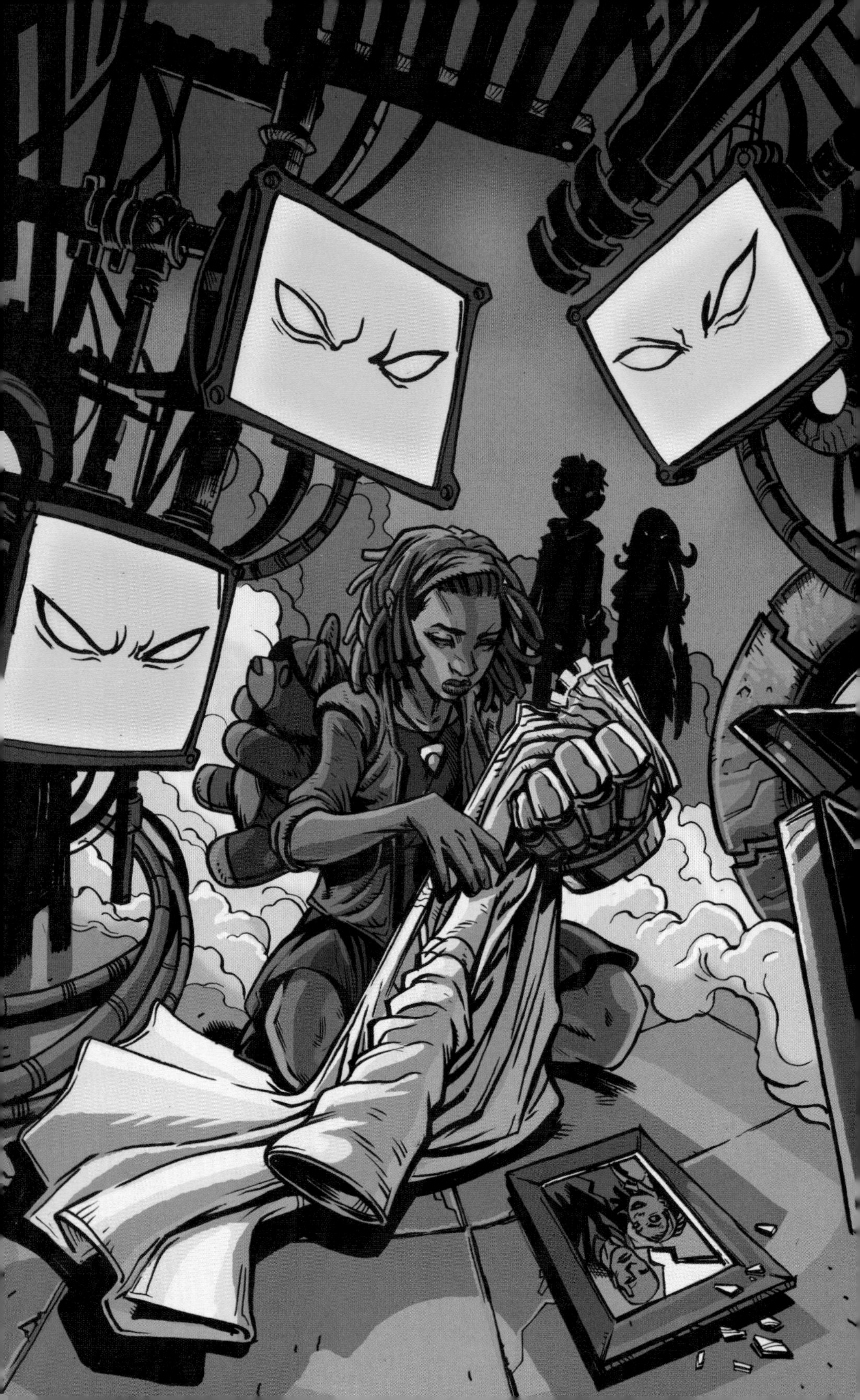

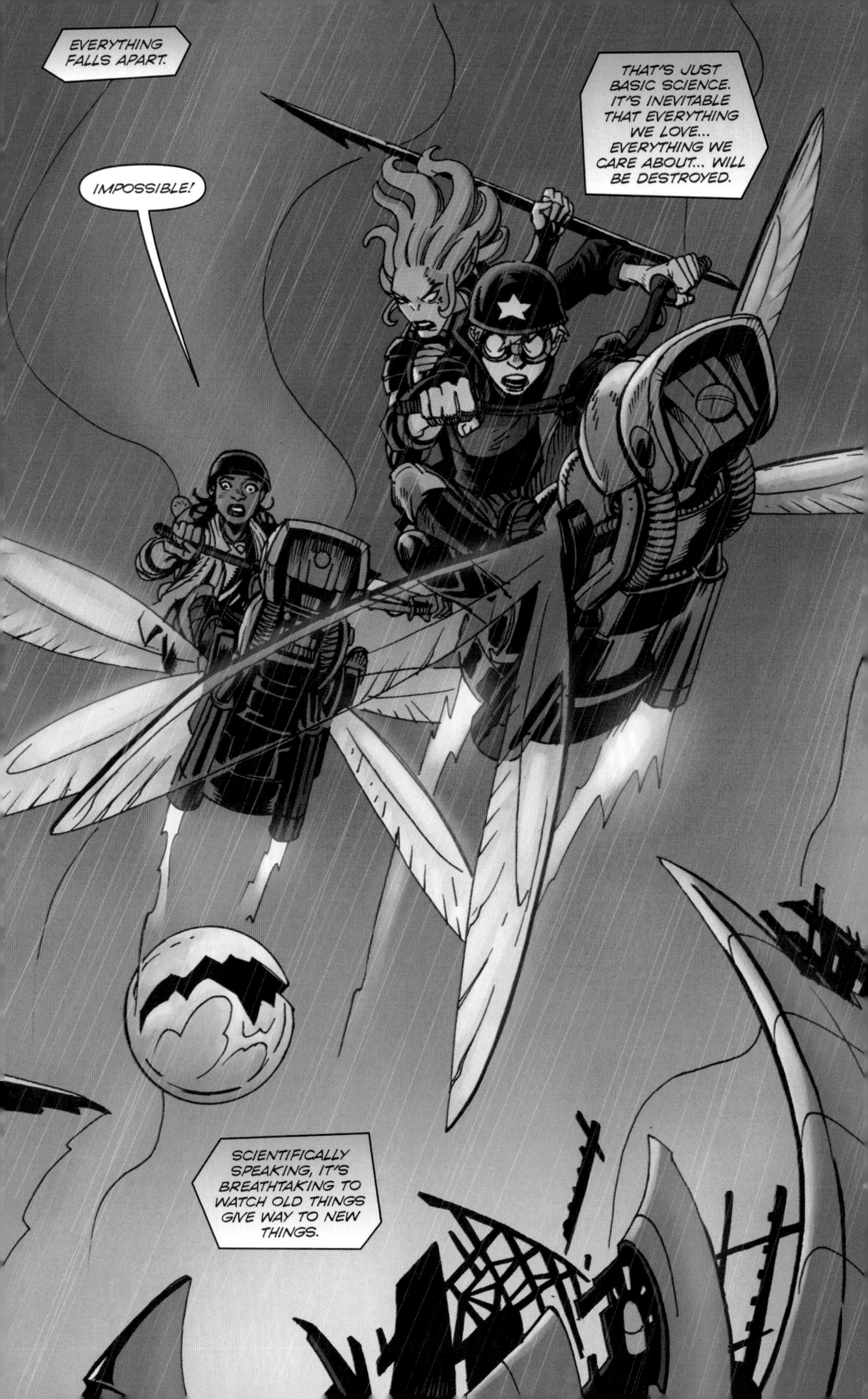
EVERYTHING FALLS APART.
IMPOSSIBLE!
THAT'S JUST BASIC SCIENCE. IT'S INEVITABLE THAT EVERYTHING WE LOVE... EVERYTHING WE CARE ABOUT... WILL BE DESTROYED.
SCIENTIFICALLY SPEAKING, IT'S BREATHTAKING TO WATCH OLD THINGS GIVE WAY TO NEW THINGS.

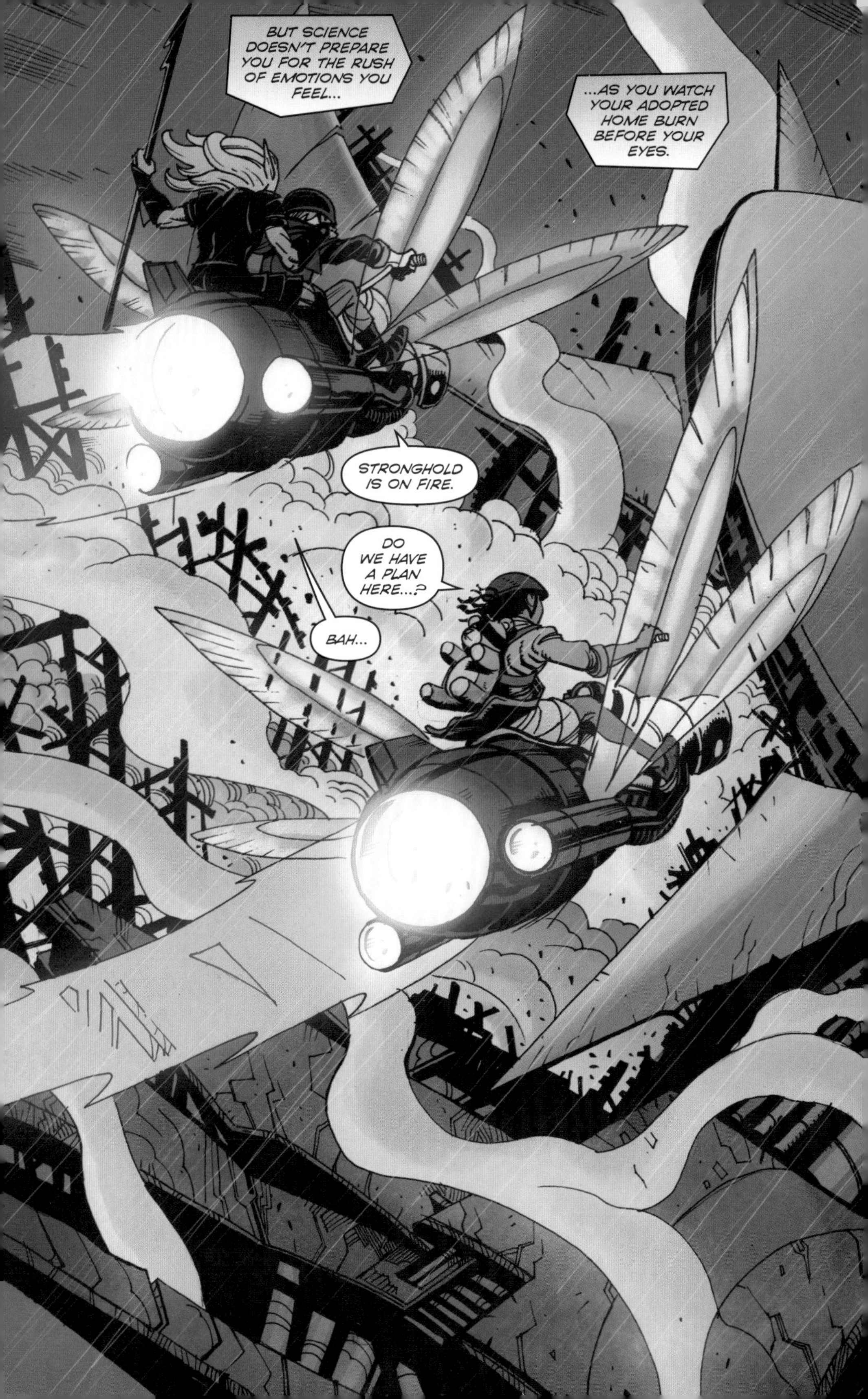
BUT SCIENCE DOESN'T PREPARE YOU FOR THE RUSH OF EMOTIONS YOU FEEL...
...AS YOU WATCH YOUR ADOPTED HOME BURN BEFORE YOUR EYES.
STRONGHOLD IS ON FIRE.
DO WE HAVE A PLAN HERE...?
BAH...

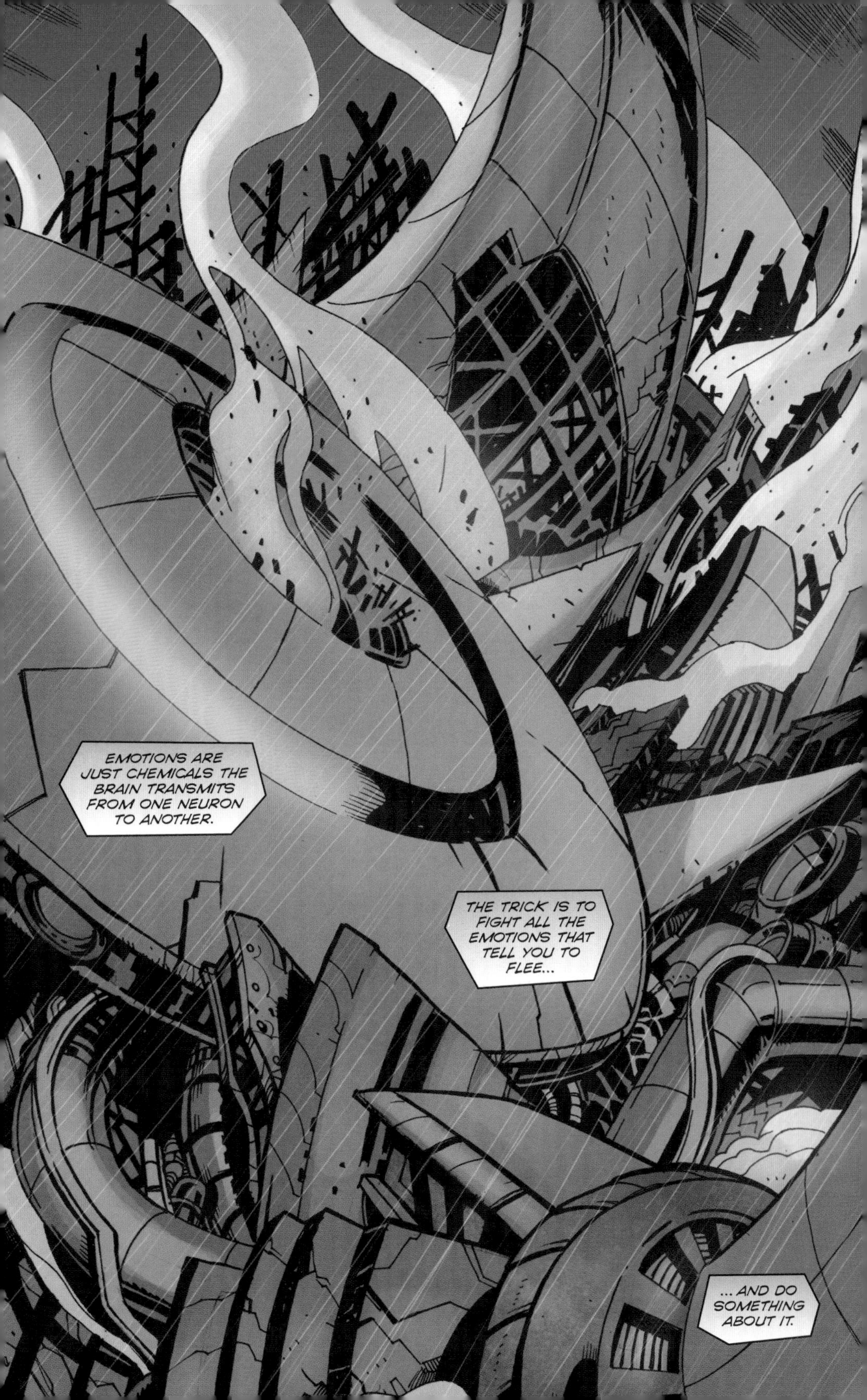
EMOTIONS ARE JUST CHEMICALS THE BRAIN TRANSMITS FROM ONE NEURON TO ANOTHER.
THE TRICK IS TO FIGHT ALL THE EMOTIONS THAT TELL YOU TO FLEE...
...AND DO SOMETHING ABOUT IT.

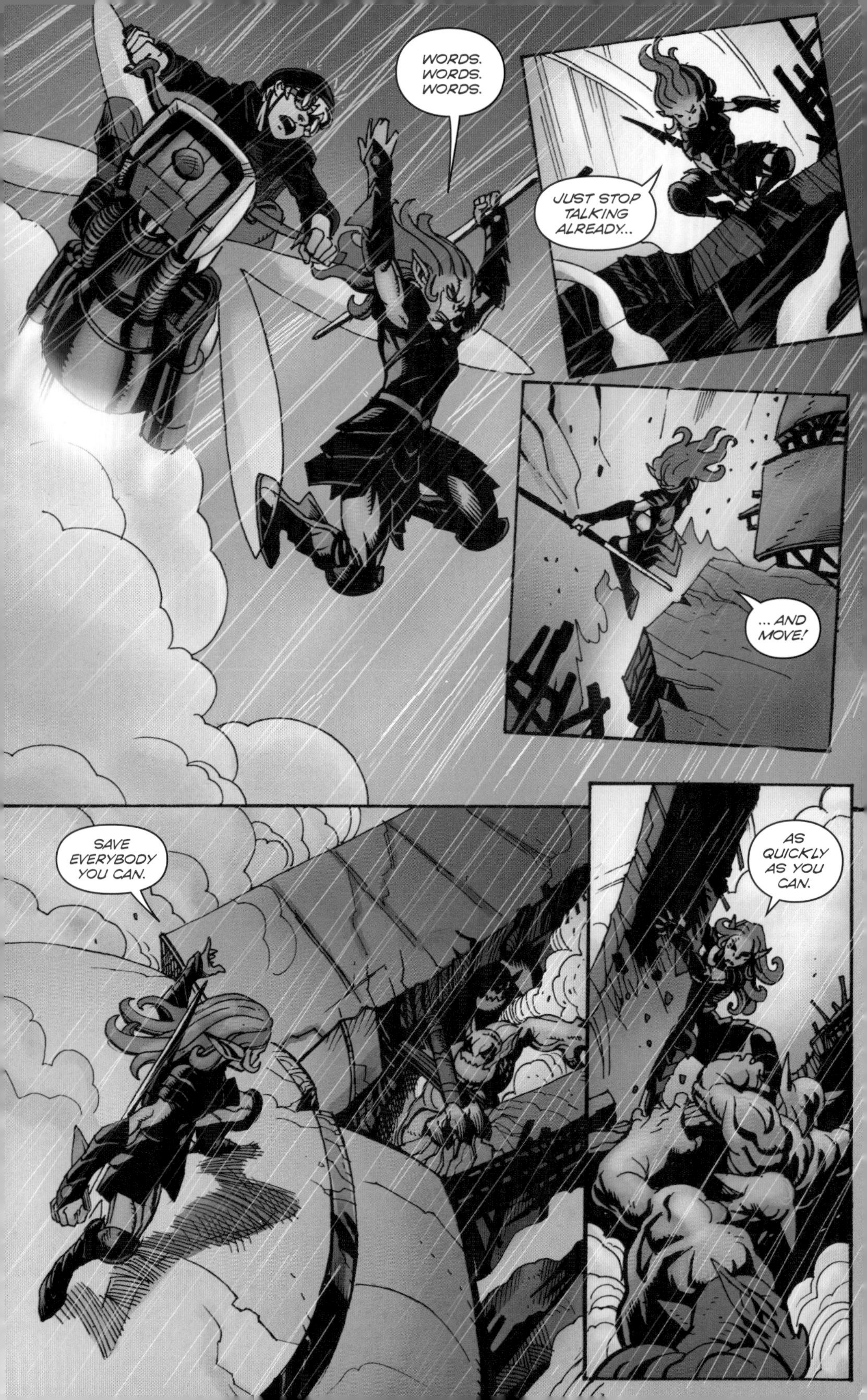
WORDS. WORDS. WORDS.
JUST STOP TALKING ALREADY...
...AND MOVE!
SAVE EVERYBODY YOU CAN.
AS QUICKLY AS YOU CAN.

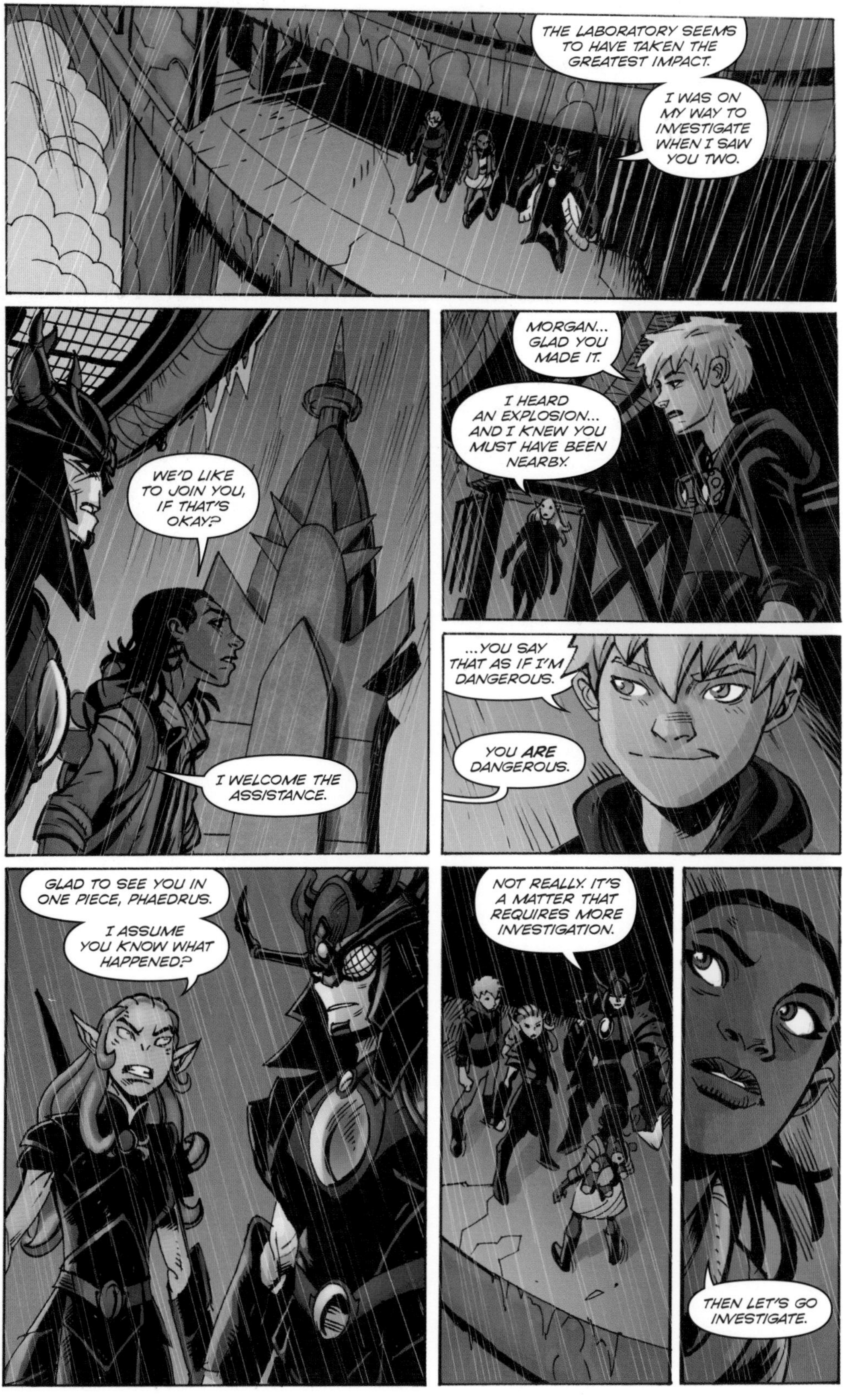
THE LABORATORY SEEMS TO HAVE TAKEN THE GREATEST IMPACT.
I WAS ON MY WAY TO INVESTIGATE WHEN I SAW YOU TWO.
WE'D LIKE TO JOIN YOU, IF THAT'S OKAY?
I WELCOME THE ASSISTANCE.
MORGAN... GLAD YOU MADE IT.
I HEARD AN EXPLOSION... AND I KNEW YOU MUST HAVE BEEN NEARBY.
...YOU SAY THAT AS IF I'M DANGEROUS.
YOU ARE DANGEROUS.
GLAD TO SEE YOU IN ONE PIECE, PHAEDRUS.
I ASSUME YOU KNOW WHAT HAPPENED?
NOT REALLY. IT'S A MATTER THAT REQUIRES MORE INVESTIGATION.
THEN LET'S GO INVESTIGATE.

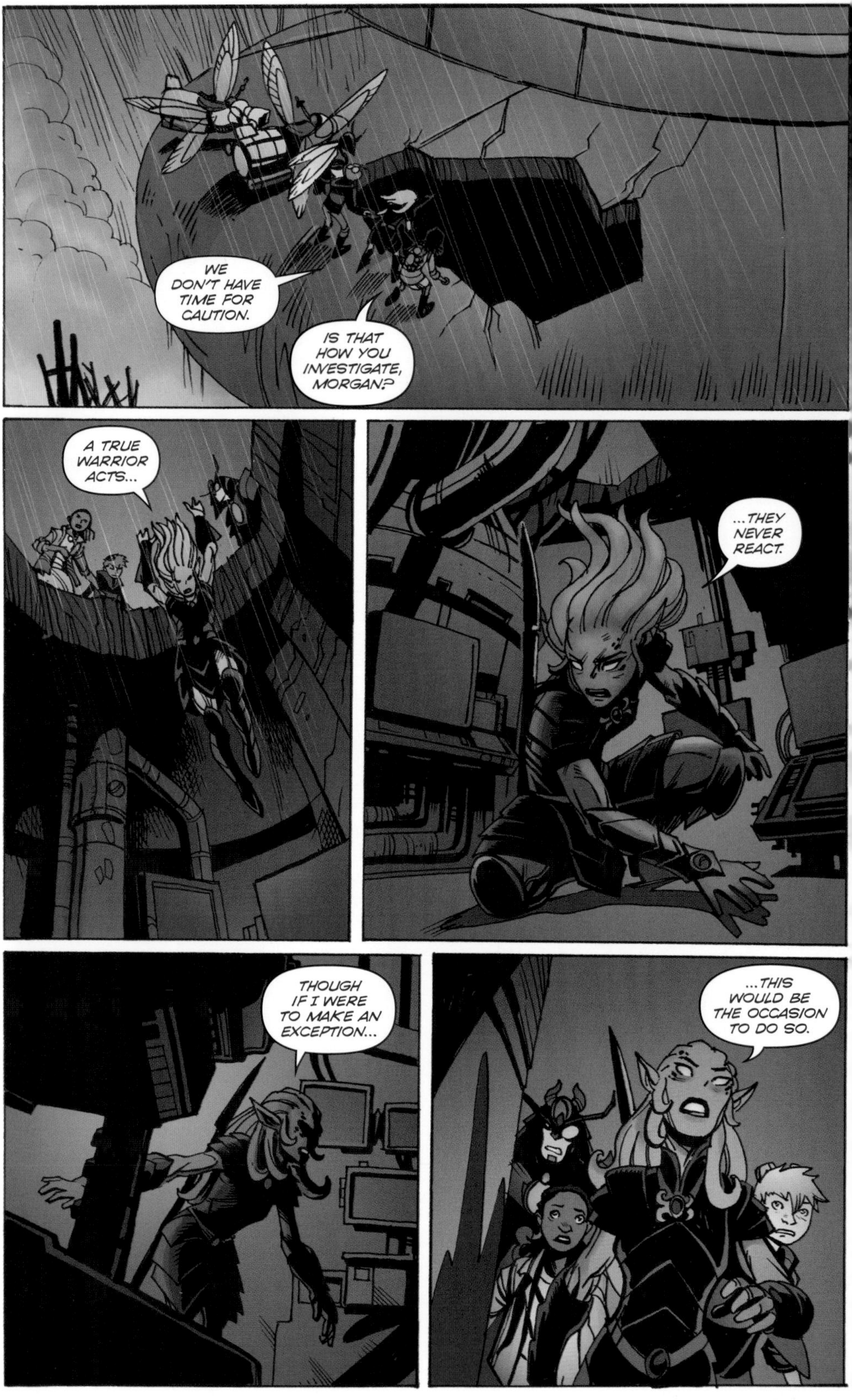
WE DON'T HAVE TIME FOR CAUTION.
IS THAT HOW YOU INVESTIGATE, MORGAN?
A TRUE WARRIOR ACTS...
...THEY NEVER REACT.
THOUGH IF I WERE TO MAKE AN EXCEPTION...
...THIS WOULD BE THE OCCASION TO DO SO.

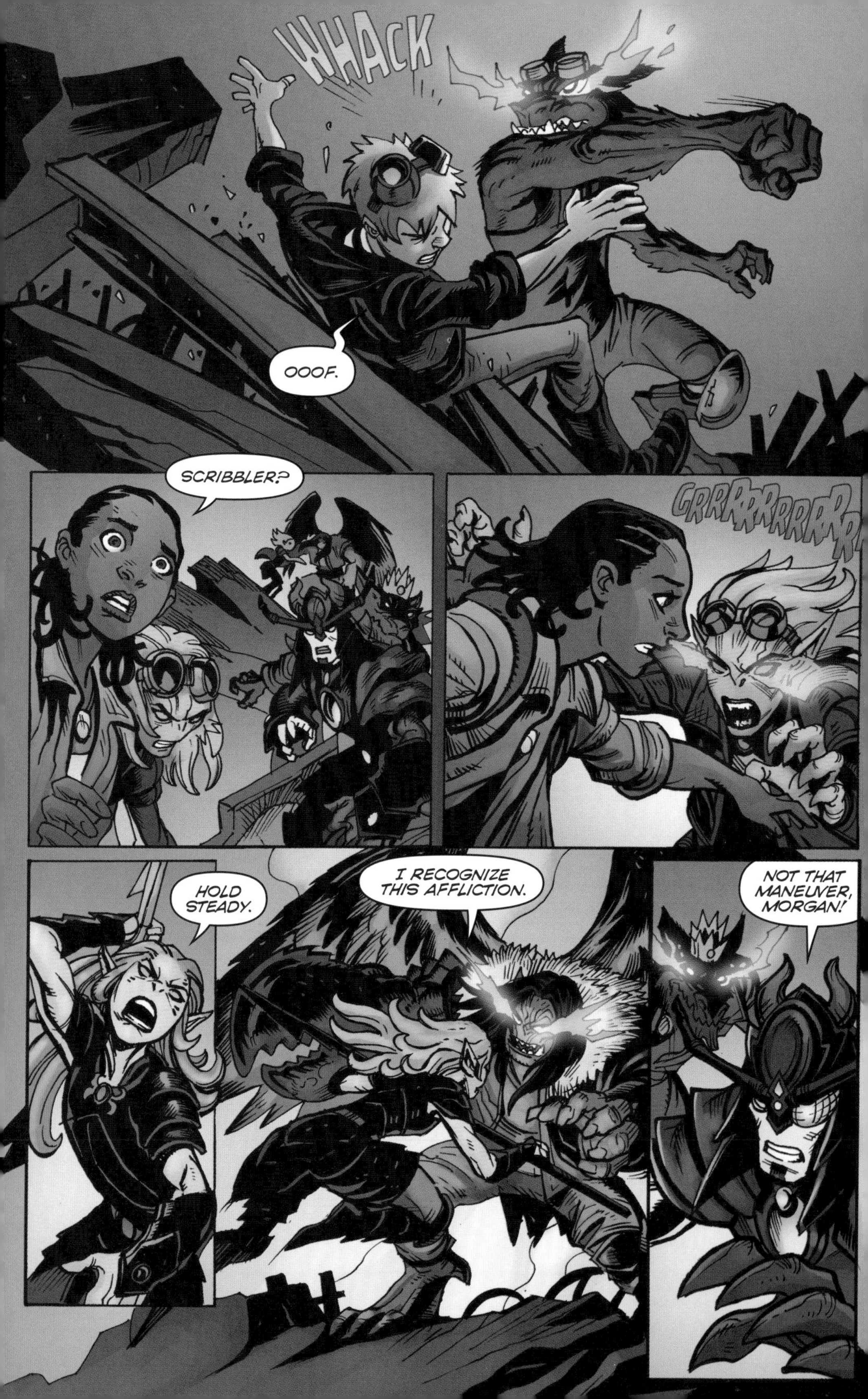
WHACK
OOOF.
SCRIBBLER?
GRRRRRRRRRRR
HOLD STEADY.
I RECOGNIZE THIS AFFLICTION.
NOT THAT MANEUVER, MORGAN!

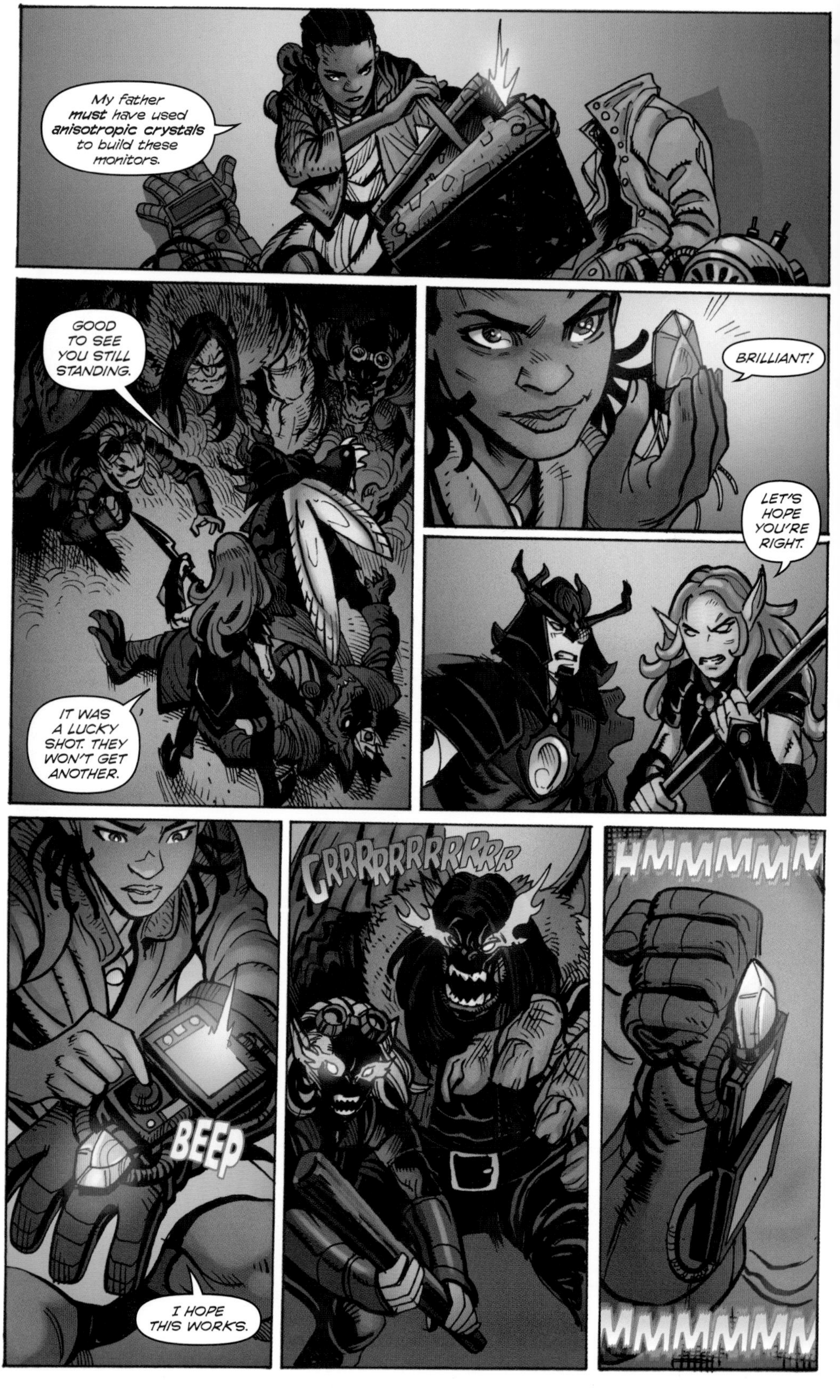
My father **must** have used **anisotropic crystals** to build these monitors.
GOOD TO SEE YOU STILL STANDING.
IT WAS A LUCKY SHOT. THEY WON'T GET ANOTHER.
BRILLIANT!
LET'S HOPE YOU'RE RIGHT.
BEEP
I HOPE THIS WORKS.
GRRRRRRRRRR
HMMMMMN
MMMMMMN

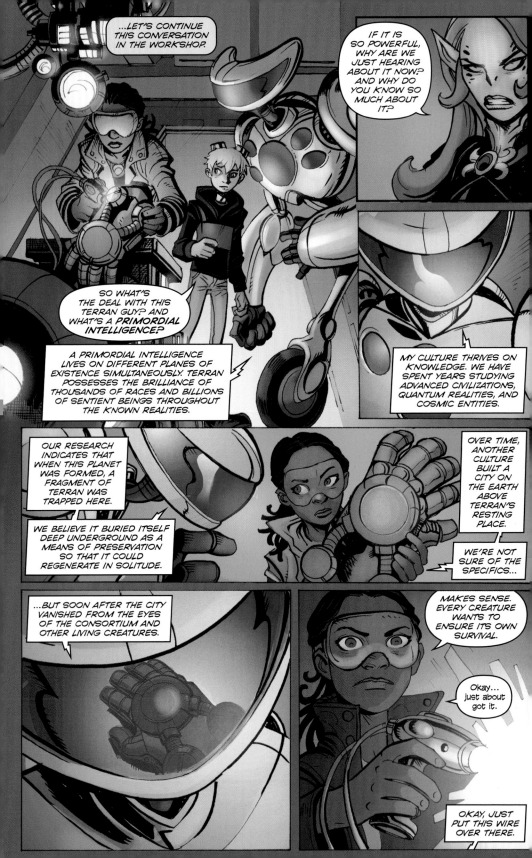

WATCH OUT FOR PAPERCUTZ™

Welcome back to the beginning! Confused? Allow me to explain. I'm Jim Salicrup, the Editor-in-Chief of Papercutz, that gung-ho group of Earthlings dedicated to publishing great graphic novels for all ages. And it seems like every day I'm told that I've got a lot of explaining to do...

While this is indeed the very first THE ONLY LIVING GIRL graphic novel, it is also a continuation of the events seen in THE ONLY LIVING BOY graphic novel series. But if you're joining us for the first time, we hope you don't feel like you walked in on the middle of a movie and don't have a clue as to what's going on. It's a tricky balancing act—bringing first-timers up-to-speed without boring long-time fans—and writer/co-creator David Gallaher and artist/co-creator Steve Ellis did a wonderful job of pulling it off. They're cleverly giving you all the information you need to follow the story in THE ONLY LIVING GIRL without spoiling all the surprises still to be found in THE ONLY LIVING BOY.

What's THE ONLY LIVING BOY and why do I keep mentioning it? To further explain, THE ONLY LIVING BOY started out as a critically-acclaimed webcomic by David Gallaher and Steve Ellis, which you can still enjoy online at www.the-only-living-boy.com. Papercutz proudly published all THE ONLY LIVING BOY comics as a series of five graphic novels, and then collected those (plus even more comics) in THE ONLY LIVING BOY OMNIBUS. And so it seemed, the epic grand adventure of twelve-year-old Erik Farrell was brilliantly concluded and all nicely wrapped up... except it wasn't. All of which finally brings us to THE ONLY LIVING GIRL, the follow-up graphic novel series that begins where THE ONLY LIVING BOY ended. See, it all makes sense now.

For those of you who have been following along since the very first Papercutz edition of THE ONLY LIVING BOY, and are looking for even more great comics by the awesome team of Gallaher and Ellis while waiting for the next ONLY LIVING GIRL graphic novel, may I suggest a very interesting project I'm sure you'll enjoy—HIGH MOON. It's a supernatural western adventure, but it's not a Papercutz graphic novel suitable for all ages. It's like a lot of R-rated films that feature a lot of gun violence, such as *The Ballad of Buster Scruggs*. So, if you're not old enough to see an R-rated movie on your own, we strongly suggest either getting your parents' permission before looking at HIGH MOON or waiting till you're at least 17-years-old.

For lighter, approved for all-ages entertainment, fans of our favorite Mermidonian warrior-woman, Morgan Dwar, may enjoy the comical tales of someone who could possibly be her long-lost cousin— GILLBERT, "The Little Merman." Created, written, drawn, colored, and lettered by the super-famous, best-selling, and award-winning cartoonist Art Baltazar. Art is known for being the creative force behind *Itty Bitty Hellboy*, *Tiny Titans*, and so many more super-cool comics. GILLBERT #1 "The Little Merman" introduces us to Gillbert, the son of King Nauticus and Queen Niadora, and his friends Albert, Sherbert, and Anne, as they all party and deal with an alien invasion.

Distant cousins?

And let's not forget the classic tale by Hans Christian Andersen that originally brought us THE LITTLE MERMAID. Papercutz proudly presents a beautiful comics adaptation by Metaphrog (the award-winning duo of John Chalmers and Sandra Marrs), that David Gallaher (remember him?) describes thusly: "With exquisite illustrations and vibrant storytelling, THE LITTLE MERMAID is a fairy tale worth believing in." It truly is a beautiful book that we're sure you'll enjoy.

Which brings us back to THE ONLY LIVING GIRL #1, which if you enjoyed it as much as we did, you're now eager to get your hands on THE ONLY LIVING GIRL #2 "Beneath the Unseen City." It'll be available soon at booksellers everywhere.

Thanks, JIM

STAY IN TOUCH!

EMAIL: salicrup@papercutz.com
WEB: papercutz.com
INSTAGRAM: @papercutzgn
TWITTER: @papercutzgn
FACEBOOK: PAPERCUTZGRAPHICNOVELS
FAN MAIL: Papercutz, 160 Broadway, Suite 700,
             East Wing, New York, NY 10038

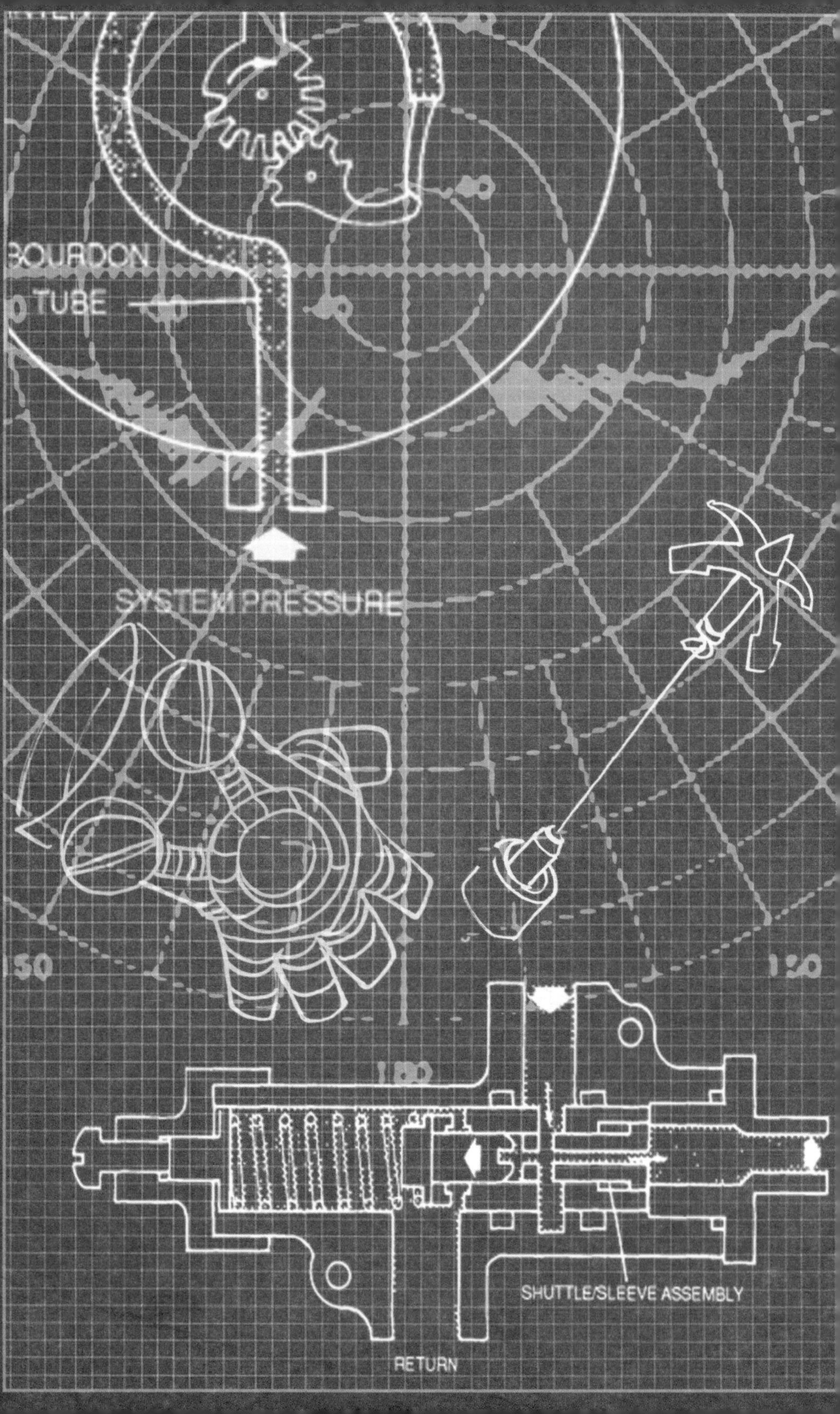
BOURDON
TUBE
SYSTEM PRESSURE
150
120
SHUTTLE/SLEEVE ASSEMBLY
RETURN